MAURYA'S SEED

MAURYA'S SEED

▼

—WHY HOPE LIVES BEHIND PROJECT WALLS

Written by C. Wright-Lewis
illustrated by Robert Derrick

Writers Club Press
New York Lincoln Shanghai

MAURYA'S SEED
—WHY HOPE LIVES BEHIND PROJECT WALLS

Writers Club Press
an imprint of iUniverse, Inc.

For information address:
iUniverse
2021 Pine Lake Road, Suite 100
Lincoln, NE 68512
www.iuniverse.com

ISBN: 0-595-19576-8

Printed in the United States of America

I dedicate this book to my children:
Thank you Cheyenne and Ademola
I could not have written this book
Without your love, encouragement and sacrificed time

ACKNOWLEDGEMENTS

First and foremost, I must give honor and gratitude to The Almighty, Most High Creator of all without whom I would not exist. Next I must thank all of my ancestors who are responsible for whispering this great story in my ear until I had no choice but to relay it to an audience, I pray that one day I learn all of your names. I thank my parents, Gwendolyn Wright and James Peterson for allowing me to re-enter the world, my brothers and sisters and the Brownsville community for molding me and placing me on their shoulders. For your unceasing love and support I thank both my biological sisters; Sherine and Judith, and my spiritual sisters Patsy, Sasteh, Ameiye,my biological children Cheyenne and Ademola, and my spiritual children, which are too many to name. I love you all.

INTRODUCTION

"AFTERMATH"

Some people came in desperateness
through consequence
by coincidence

while others came by hopelessness
some hope-fullness
via homelessness,
but I was born in Brownsville.

Some people left in wealthiness
through stealthiness
by filthiness

while others escaped or dared to try
by getting high
on liquid sky,
but I was groomed in Brownsville.

Some made it out, a righteous route
without a doubt
though quite a bout

Then vowed that once upon the track
not to come back
nor ever to be black,
but my home will always be Brownsville.

Never wishing to flee, like a well-rooted tree
a simple woman and man
the fire to fan
stayed behind and took the stand.

The hope of ancestors, hold our future in their hearts
tend the garden in the projects, ever- healing ailing parts.
With my assistance, we'll erase the pain
destroy the disdain, and reattach the chain.
It's time I return to Brownsville.

C. Wright-Lewis 9/92

Chapter One

"Aftermath"

BROWNS' VILLAGE
July 2000

Tres (Tray) was losing the battle against the black Lexus on his left as he awaited the green light. He was struggling to hear his new oldies station and the Lexus was blasting gangsta rap. The beat was hot, but the words were vulgar, Tres just couldn't tolerate it. He didn't hate rap, just the vulgarity and the sex songs with no creativity, poetry or purpose. His sons looked up at him wincing with apprehension because they knew how he felt about "the songs with no damn point."

"You see that brother?" he pointed at the car inching ahead of him, "he's trying his best to live his life like the rapper on the song. And the rapper doesn't even live like that. Don't be a sucker. You can have a fly car and a job that won't land you in jail."

He stared into the eyes of the driver to show his fearlessness before the Lexus shot out in front of him with a screech and a howl.

The two boys were shaking their heads and staring intensely at their dad.

"We're gonna see a lot of that today."

He parked his Ford Escort on the corner of Sutter Avenue and Powell Street.

"All right y'all, come on out and check out my old neighborhood. This…" Tres couldn't finish as he began to look around. Half excited and half repulsed, he let his young sons run in the grass behind his old building as he leaned against his car and inhaled.

Browns' Village had sunk to a new low. It was now a completely different world from the one Tres had left back in 1980 when Passion died. At least then, many of the old families were still around and they still loved their home. It was 20 years ago when Tres and his two younger sisters, Mecca and Zaire had run for their lives after cocaine dealers had broken into their apartment, destroyed every piece of furniture and appliance they owned, then shot and killed their mother, Passion.

After a life of community work and sacrifice, Passion had died as she had lived—protecting her people. In an effort to save the life of her daughter Mecca's best friend, a girl she had known from birth named Ausari, Passion had given the young woman temporary shelter. She was 21 years old and being coerced into stashing cocaine by her boyfriend and was too ashamed to go home to her spiritual parents. The boyfriend and his hoodlum friends had taken over Ausari's apartment, but she had given the drugs to Passion.

Passion and the girls had decided not to tell Tres because they hoped to resolve the problem before he got home, besides, he would have been furious to know they had endangered their lives. Tres was an intern at St. Vincent's Hospital in Manhattan, but still felt more comfortable living in Browns' Village. It was 1980 and the community which had solely survived on the soul of its people and their faith that God, hard work and good White people would give them peace, justice and the pursuit of happiness had descended into the abyss of urban plight. He planned to move Passion out the projects soon, but she was reluctant to go. All of her children harassed her daily trying to make her see how dangerous Browns' Village had become, but she just couldn't leave. To her, it was like surrendering to the enemy. But, it was apparent,

"The enemy has won! Whites will always own and operate Browns' Village. And they plan to eliminate justice and passion forever." Tres would tell her each time they discussed it. But Passion wasn't afraid of drug dealers or Nazis, Klansmen nor niggers; and that's what she would reply before she would add, "And I'm not moving!"

But this last mission was a mistake for Passion to accept. She had called her close friend, a Black peace officer and fellow community protector named David Walker and he was on his way. But the drug dealers moved in on her quicker than she expected. Passion didn't think these young, hooded-thugs were so serious about their business and she had no idea that the brown-colored, uncut cocaine she had hidden beneath the old blankets and quilts she stored in Justice's old army trunk was worth $150,000.00 on the street.

Tres remembered receiving word at the hospital that his mother had been shot dead. It nearly killed him too. The murderers left Passion's body lying like a broken doll amongst the rubble, but they had taken Ausari. Her body was found floating in the Canarsie Bay.

He and his sisters left discreetly and relocated to Queens with Miss Hannah, their parents' old friend. Then they moved to Virginia with their grandfather and planned to never look back, until today.

The new millennium had brought him back to his past and his people. And it was unfortunately clear that they had rapidly lost the war against drugs and were consistently losing their sons to New York's penal system. It seemed everyone's little brother was living on Riker's Island. And while they were there, they only learned to be angry, bitter men and better criminals. The continual loss of family members to heroin and prison over the last 40 years had caused the village to crumble. Sadly, it was worse than Tres ever imagined it could become. It was not so much the appearance of his old neighborhood. It didn't appear to be devastated like it was back in the seventies after riots and drug trafficking had made it the city's highest crime area. New stores had been built, and additional, affordable housing was available. But, the base of building walls were a dead, dirty white and covered with coded, colorless graffiti adults couldn't understand, opposed to the colorful African images that once lifted the spirit of the entire neighborhood. Drug addicts now lined the corners closest to the methadone clinic during the weekdays, always leaving trails of crack vials, hypodermic needles and other drug paraphernalia for Browns' Village's residents to step over on their way home from the Sutter Avenue station every evening.

Gates had been built around the housing complex where Tres and his younger brother Deuce once ruled on the basketball courts. Police now harassed any male, Black or Latino, on a daily basis, demanding proof of residence and identity- just like in South Africa.

Poverty reigned over Browns' Village, though Tres couldn't tell by the outward appearance of most people; it was a new kind of poverty. Even those who had to live under the welfare system had become so brainwashed by materialistic values, they dressed their children better than they fed their children. Principles of morality had lost the war to principles of commercialism to the point where some sold drugs just to wear labels bearing the names of people who could care less about them. More grandparents and government programs were raising children than mothers and fathers. And as if there weren't enough problems, gangs had migrated from California and recruited the weak-hearted few who weren't in jail.

Politicians used the neighborhood to host homeless shelters, juvenile detention centers, drug rehabilitation centers and any other state or federal program city residents of any other ethnicity would protest against being in their own back yards. Day Care Centers were located right across the street from methadone centers and men's homeless shelters. Public schools in Browns' Village continued the tradition of having the lowest reading and math scores in the city since the sixties. Enraged, organized tenant patrol members picketed and marched against the injustices against Browns' Village but had finally given up after losing year after year.

Keeping his sons within his peripheral vision, Tres glanced down Sutter Avenue into his childhood and could see himself walking to church with his surrogate grandmother, Mama Lettie–his hand in hers–swinging to the beat of their favorite song, *"swing low, sweet chariot coming for to carry me hoome,"* in a 2/4 swing beat. The voices of old sang over in his head, but reality raped the reminiscence. Folks still went to church on Sunday, yet Sunday had somehow lost its sacredness. One hardly ever saw little children dressed in their Sunday best, holding hands with their parents as they walked to the neighborhood sanctuary. Gospel music no longer awakened the entire neighborhood as it had years ago and accompanied the churchgoers down Sutter Avenue. Stores were now opened every day of the week and people shopped and worked just as if Sunday was any other day.

Gone was the mouth-watering smell of breakfast from Murray's Coffee Shop on the corner of Sutter and Powell, where early Sunday morning risers stopped for a light breakfast they shared with those who slept in, but lived a quick inhalation away. The smell of his famous salmon cakes and sweet corn muffins were unfortunately replaced with the stench of uncollected trash piled up on the corner, stale urine-stained walls and back doorways used as toilets, mixed with the acrid smell of crack being smoked in unlit staircases.

The flavor of Browns' Village had changed. The spirit was gone. And, the love had turned to stone now that Passion and Justice were dead.

Tres took his boys by the hand. He had come back on the anniversary of the community center his parents once run; he had accepted the invitation to make a short speech and accept an award on their behalf. It had been a long time, and he was curious to see how the community had changed, if at all. Since his sons were 11 and 12, the same age as he and his brother were when they last played on Sutter Avenue almost 30 years ago, he had a strange desire to allow them to see his childhood home. Tres had always described his parents to his sons as heroes and promised to show them the memorial built for the much loved and missed Justice Freeman Jr. and Passion Freeman in front of the Browns' Village community center one day. They loved hearing stories about their grandfather–the one-handed djembe drummer and his beautiful wife, Passion. But of all the stories Tres would tell them late at night before bed, their favorites were about their great-grandfather Papa Joe.

The adventurous escapades Tres and Deuce had with Papa Joe in The Dew Drop Inn in Browns' Village had convinced them that their great-grandfather was the most intrepid and intriguing hero of all times. But since they only knew him as an 85 year old, who incidentally still ran his own record shop in Newport News, they were amazed to hear of the things he did in his youth. He had taken care of his great-grands in the shop every Saturday morning from the time they could use the john; it had been their special time together. But, he had suddenly taken ill and died last winter, and they missed him terribly. Their Papa Joe had been bigger than life, but had happily knelt on the floor with them to play army soldiers or would put on '45's and taught them to do the twist.

They would have never imagined the number of lives their Papa Joe had touched and changed as a father of a community. Like Moses and Harriet Tubman, Papa Joe had created a secret passageway for Blacks still chained to oppressing sharecropping contracts as far south as the Delta to escape to Browns' Village. He had started the movement in 1963 after a trip to Mississippi when he learned that slavery was still in existence, but was shut down by 1968 when Dr. King was assassinated. Before that day, he had saved hundreds and exposed locations of working plantations and factories owned by descendants of former slave owners throughout the south. Before it was all over, Papa Joe, the communal family and journalists who were dedicated to the struggle for equality, had succeeded in immobilizing free labor in America and robbing a few southern aristocrats out of several million dollars. The boys couldn't wait to hear what people in Browns' Village had to say about their beloved ancestor.

He used to reminisce about Browns' Village almost everyday before he died and would have loved to come back, but the Browns' Village of 2000 would have broken Papa Joe's heart. His life in Browns' Village had preceded projects, welfare and drug lords. His love for this community was founded on the fact that even before Blacks migrated to Browns' Village and it was a predominantly Jewish neighborhood, it was known to be financially impoverished, yet culturally rich, and Papa Joe had been a part of its bounty. Now his children's children had returned to rekindle the flame of hope in the community where education and equality once meant more than wealth. It had meant freedom.

Patrick and Justice Freeman IV, who their parents had nick-named Pat and Quarter, stood behind the fourteen story building their father called home with their bent necks and squinting eyes neglecting to reveal the top floors they desperately tried to see.

"I've never seen a building this tall Pat. I wonder what it's like to live on the top floor."

Patrick was looking at his father who was taking paint cans out of the car.

"Well I don't get it. Exactly what is so special about Browns' Village, Quarter?'

"I don't know, but I think were going to find out today."

"DAWN"—

"LOVE WARRIORS"

Embracing the battlefield daily at dawn
their halos hidden
Adorned in amorous armor
Prepared through prayer and praise
March the love warriors

Divinely drafted, trained through their trials
their scars forgotten
Inspired in spirit
Bathed in bravery of word and bond
March the love warriors

All is what they must conquer
Everyone, who they must combat
Conquerors for they have already won
Confident for they bleed with His blood
His spirit's in their bones, resurrection's to come

"Go ye therefore" to the front line
Fear no man nor naught
Strike fiercely with agape
kill hatred and ought

who are the love warriors?
I'm sure you know two

The Creator's catalysts
Who help us all through

Unconcerned with compensation
Life is their job
Field workers with passion
who often are robbed

Prayer answerers unaware of all they've allowed
Blessings bestowed through sweat of their brow
Yet, blessed themselves though concerned of it not
Giving and loving gratifies this strange lot

Embracing the battlefield, not only at dawn
not only when strengthened, sometimes they are worn
Yet, adorned in love
armed in awesome faith
they March
March on, March on Love Warriors.

                                        Cathie W-Lewis

Chapter Two

▼

"Dawn"

BROWNS' VILLAGE
July 17, 1963
6:00 A.M.

Passion awoke having left where she was about to go. She had just escaped the boycott; but bloody cops and burning buildings from the prophetic nightmare continued to appear before her now opened eyes. She smiled, recalling the shocked looks on white faces from seeing more black people than they had ever imagined existed in their segregated lives.

She had seen the riot, felt the maniacal pain, heard the piercing screams and she had wanted Justice. As usual, she could feel him within her as she awakened, so the pain of loss was not stinging today as it sometimes would. The yellow buses rolled across what she couldn't decipher as her memory's dream or her dream's memory, as Passion sat up in bed. Her thick eyebrows fought consciousness and forced her eyes shut again. The vision returned.

White folks with picket signs–visible anger–opened mouths–red faces. Visible heat. Rising heat on the left, a castle-like school building–fire. The yellow buses circled the burning school; the wagon train prepared for the attack. Children screamed for, "Mama!" and "Equality!" and "JESUS!" The cries formed into black and white blocks of clouds and hovered over the crumbling welcome sign proudly worn by Whitestone Public Elementary School, which claimed–"Only the Best for Our Children". It burned, but didn't singe, then it crumbled and transformed into black and white snowflakes, which joined with the clouds of cries and slowly blanketed the crowd while it smothered the fire. Passion watched herself watching the strange snowfall to the ground, but when she raised her head, before her stood the bloody cop again. He was holding the body of a bloody, black boy whose face she couldn't make out. She began to scream aloud.

Then realizing her four sleeping children could hear her, she quickly covered her mouth. She tried to calm her heaving chest before they would enter her bedroom, believing she had called them by name. Deuce, her tallest, though youngest son entered, and kissed her all over her face, "Good Morning Mama, Mama, Mama, Mama"; between each "Mama" a kiss was planted north, south, east and west on her face. This was their private ritual. She did the same to each of her children when they were babies, but Deuce was the only one who remembered and reciprocated–daily. Relieved her voice hadn't frightened them all, she held him over her thumping heart and momentarily closed her eyes.

"How's my big man this morning?" she rubbed his short-cropped afro and smiled with delight. He looked just like his dad. "Get the ball rolling for me, brother–today's the day. Get your brother and sisters out of bed and start breakfast," she sweetly requested as consciousness finally coerced her out of bed; her request was translated to "Put on WWRL" in Deuce language. He loved waking up first and blasting the radio to wake his siblings, who loved it in return. He ran to the living room to seize the stereo system. Passion prayed, but *"Sugar pie honey bunch, you know that I love you...I can't help myself, I love you and nobody else,"* caused her to rush the "Amen". Thoughts of what this day would bring still had Passion's heart beating loudly, "I trust God," she whispered to herself and stepped into the bathroom. The cool shower simmered her fire and returned her thoughts to Justice. She could smell him. She could still smell him and it still made her feel the heaven within her. Remembering she'd never feel his body again just caused extended lingering under the hot sprinkles.

His eyes had been entrancing; at times she swore she could feel them watching her. Like anyone else who had ever been in his presence, she couldn't help seeing those light brown eyes even when they were long gone. Anyone who had talked to Justice had felt Justice. When he looked you in the eyes, you could see his soul, and he could see yours too. Looking into Justice's eyes was like looking at love. One could see his love for Passion in Justice's eyes. Or, you could see the best picture of your own self in Justice's eyes because the reflection that Justice gave of everyone was what he saw in each person—their divine uniqueness. Pure love. Unanimously, it was always an enjoyable experience. Everyone had loved Justice in return, but not like Passion. She slowly inhaled his image and stepped into the day.

When Passion Franklin married Justice Freeman Jr., she also married his vision, his passion for his village and all those who loved him. It wasn't that Passion didn't already love her people. Of course she did. She naturally did that right along with loving herself, who she was and where her people were from; the pride in the apparent tenacity of her African descendants oozed from Passion's pores and manifested through the scents of lavender and lotus blossom that always entered a room before her. That's what he had first loved about her the most—her scent, her natural beauty. After they grew together, *her* passion and wit impressed him most.

It was natural that Passion and Justice's energy locked early. Passion was only 13 and Justice 15 years old when they first started "going together." Everyone watched them growing closer day by day. They had become inseparable. Although the neighbor's warned their parents to "watch those two," the reverend and Joseph Justice learned that they only made things worse when forbidding them to see one another. It was obviously more than puppy love. So it came as no surprise to all of Browns' Village when they were married with one son in Justice's arms and another ready to enter the world three shorts years after their first kiss. The new family was a rare second generation of native New Yorkers of southern descent.

In this section of Browns' Village, the residents were mostly North Carolina born and came up north in the late 40's and the 50's to get jobs and "make it". Browns' Village was just to be a pit stop too, 'cause they all had big dreams. New York City was known as the greatest city in the world anyone could live and they each had every intention of living "high on the hog." Up here the opportunities were better. "Go Up North and you could make you some money, honey," they had all heard. The schools were better. The homes were better. Life was better. The white folks were even better. It was also falsely believed, "ain't even no Klan in New York." In 1953, colored people had started making great changes too. Many relatives who had been left in the South still arose at 4 a.m. to go into the field, unable to attend school or stay in school because everyone in the family was required to work in order to help out. Going to school was the answer, and it had been known all along. Living in New York City provided the African descendants with that right. "'Git your education!" echoed in the hearts of those who knew all too well, "You won't git no where without no education". Passion and Justice heard it just as all of their friends who all had parents from one North or South Carolinian city or another, and they were all expected to go to school and make something of themselves. They were not "to be caught dead being no servants, nursing Miss Anne's baby or holding open Mister Charlie's car door."

After graduating from high school, Justice went into the service. His dad, Papa Joe had served in the Marines and felt Justice would earn good money from the mechanical skills he'd learn there as well. Sadly, after encountering action he was never prepared for, Justice would return home two long years later missing a hand. Disability was good to him financially, but losing his ability to play the drum had hurt Justice intensely; he couldn't even discuss it. Viet Nam wasn't popular yet, but Justice told all about the countless troops being sent to "Nam" and the rumors of a draft. He talked late and long to a different audience almost every night, sometimes in his home, sometimes outside on the corner between doo-wopping, but mostly down at The Dew Drop Inn—Papa Joe's record shop, which doubled as the clandestine headquarters for the Brotherhood, a self-protection club which Papa Joseph Justice Freeman had started. An old warrior in spirit, he was just as dedicated to the duty of protecting the village as when he vowed to the honor over 30 years before. Justice's mother had died while giving birth to their only son. Papa Joe was in Korea at the time. He returned home to find an empty house. Lettie, Mattie, Ernestine and Jenny Mae Brown had been at Ruby's side and in the African-American tradition, they promised to raise her son, helping Joseph Justice when and however it was needed.

The Dew Drop Inn was across the street and right down the block from the apartment building where his son's family now resided. Justice and Passion's was one of the first families to move into the new city-owned housing development, which everyone consulted considered a step up out of the tenements and cold water flats most colored folks lived in if they couldn't afford a house. Many of these new housing developments were being built in Browns' Village at this time. For some reason, Browns' Village was the chosen spot. Affordable housing. Brand new. Fourteen stories high. Elevators, brand new refrigerators, stoves, bathrooms with showers. "Shoot. Some folk down south still have to use out-houses," many responded. This was indeed the good life their parents had desired and expected for their children and themselves. Three and four bedroom affordable apartments. Free maintenance. Luxury short of a doorman and a limo. Things had really changed for the race—so it was thought.

After volunteering at the Veterans Hospitals part-time, Justice spent most of his day with his children—those born to him and those bonded through community. His world took on new life whenever he stepped into the Community Center where he taught the children about their heritage and culture while playing his djembe drum, one-handed. Passion's memory of her slain husband was often envisioned with him "cheezin'", as she used to say, and holding his djembe with his handless arm. She fought the thought of his embrace in order to leave the shower, dress and greet their other children. She could still smell him. "Umf, you and your eyes", she thought, "I guess you're hanging with me today baby. Thanks, I'm sure gonna need you."

After checking the children's gettin' ready status and starting breakfast, Passion found herself at the kitchen window trying to hold on to the slight, dark, incoming breeze, as if she knew it would be a long pause before another would come to comfort her. One of her ears was captivated by, "Try a Little Tenderness," but before she could even see them, the other ear picked up the sound of the approaching yellow buses. "Here we go," she thought aloud. Punctual personnel for the 6 a.m. shift glided towards the nearby factory in the breeze and caught her attention. Passion watched the newsstand open, and she could smell coffee brewing from the luncheonette across the street that always opened at 5 to accommodate the early shifters. Eastwardly, Passion peered from her fourth floor kitchen window; the laced curtain borders blew sweetly in the fading, dark morning wind. Horizontal streaks of deep red-orange, then orange-gold, then golden yellow lifted the heat and bright light of the day. As always, she faced the sun rising over the small commercial buildings and residential multiple dwellings, and listened to the rhythmic elevator trains playing a back beat to the sputtering city buses which today escorted the long-awaited yellow buses chosen to provide the ride to freedom. It was already 70 degrees and Monday with its usual bluesy moon energy had just shoved the solemness of Sunday out of reach. But before departing, the scent of the air suddenly changed and Passion couldn't breathe. All of the city sounds and smells ceased for a second, causing her to freeze in thought and movement. She could feel the perplexed look on her face and decided not to try and change it. She closed her eyes and listened. No particular voice was heard, yet an apparent intensity of consciousness and courage came. Passion's shoulders immediately rode back, her eyes stretched without effort and her heart seemed to calm itself into a deep, slow beat, moving in perfect time with her breathing.

"GOOD MORNING MOMMYYY!" the young voices sang loudly with love, bringing her back. "You ready Ma?" that was Passion's clone–5 year old Mecca, who had begged to go along with her mother. "I wanna go Ma, I ain't scared," she reminded Passion who didn't verbally respond, just gave that look that tells any child, "Don't even go there!"

The morning activity heightened within seconds, but Passion flowed with it all. The phone rang, Mama Lettie began banging on the front door, believing it was necessary to compete with WWRL which was now playing Aretha's new hit. Passion wondered if it had been on all along.

"Paat, Paat. ...PASSIONN!!", the Spanish accent bellowed from the street below. All of her friends had called Passion Pat for short, everyone but Justice.

"Don't be cutting my Passion short, "he had always joked.

She could still smell him. She even thought she heard him earlier, during the timelessness. She floated back in time for a moment envisioning them at the kitchen table playing bid whist as she and Justice often did. He would infuriate their challengers by talking across the table to her, "You know what card to play," he'd say, and she always played the right one.

"Hmmm.," she thought aloud. Anne was on the phone. Deuce had picked it up, and as he did, Passion could see Anne's face in the dream. Anne would be key today and Passion was already proud of her. "That's my girl." she thought and smiled while heading to the door. Mama Lettie was growing impatient. Tres, her oldest son, was at the window.

"Good Morning Miss Connie, where's Eddie? He goin'? Mama said we couldn't go." Eddie, Connie's oldest, and Deuce were the same age and were supposed to be in the same class at this new school they had to fight to attend.

"Good morning Poppi, where's you mother?, Eddie is staying home too. You'll see him later.

"Mama's on the phone I think."

"Tell her I'm back from the bakery; I'm ready whenever she is!"

"Okay Miss Connie, tell Eddie I'll see him at the park at lunchtime!"

Mama Lettie was attacked by the girls as soon as she stepped in the door. They almost knocked down the beautiful quilt off the wall. Passion's mother had given it to her after she had given birth to Tres. The heirloom had geometric shapes of royal blue mixed with sky and sea blues, and although there were no identifiable bodies within the interwoven cloth, brown shapes of anguish seemed to be fleeing something evil in the sea. The odd, but creative hand-made designs caught your attention and remained with one's memory forever. It was really something to see, and the very first thing to grasp you as you entered into Passion's home. Peace, and the presence of advising, protective ancestors were strongly felt. Another attention grabber, was a 1920's keepsake, a beautiful hand fan designed with black angels she had encased in glass above a living room chair; a jumped broom hung in another corner, and a china cabinet filled with crystal-framed pictures of aunts, grandmothers and fathers, Passion and Justice's parents, and elders dating back to the late 1800's. The entire apartment was painted the palest blue, and at sunrise, when the natural light kissed it, it appeared a heavenly white. Passion never missed a sunrise. As the day progressed, and the sun took shade within, the room was just as inviting. Incense of cedar, frank and myrrh, or sandalwood permeated daily throughout the apartment, and it was always peaceful.

"Y'all be careful out there today..." Mama Lettie had started before she realized Passion was on the phone. She began dishing out the grits and eggs Passion had cooked. Mecca, Zaire and, of course Deuce, who was always the first to the table, quickly sat down. They began to question Mama Lettie about the protest.

"You going to the march too Mama Lettie?" Little Zaire asked, planting her elbows on the table and her fists tucked under her chin to show her disappointment.

"No, I'm staying right here with you. And, it's not really a march baby, it's a rally–a protest rally."

"Cause the white people don't want us to git our education, right Mama Lettie?" Mecca was proud of the knowledge she had attained from listening to her mother.

"That's right. But all y'all are gonna get the best education possible 'cause that's your right. And can't nobody take it away from you–not without a fight. Right!"

"Yes Mama Lettie!" they all chimed.

"We still want to go Mama Lettie, tell Mama to let us go." She was shaking her head slightly from side to side, understanding their desire, but also Passion's fear. "You just said it's for our education–our rights. As the oldest, Tres was always the appointed spokesman.

Mama Lettie listened to the end of the phone call and shushed the children, knowing Passion wasn't about to change her mind. They had both sensed danger and felt it was best that the girls attend their Summer Day Camp Program. Deuce and Tres had begun working with Papa Joe at The Dew Drop Inn. So they didn't really protest too loudly. Money meant comic books and new 45's. They all had been to rallies before, but once Medgar Evers was just killed; Passion just didn't feel as comfortable about taking her children along.

"All right," Passion sang, trying to end the phone call, "All right Sis, I'll meet you in front of the church at 7:30, we're rolling at 8."

Mama Lettie looked both ways as if checking for oncoming traffic, making Passion and the kids laugh.

"Y'all be careful out there", she safely began again, "Them crackers ain't no joke you know, they ain't gonna take this lying down". Passion nodded seriously. Mama Lettie was always good for a joke for the sake of levity, but she was worried today. She had had a few dreams of her own, and a few nightmares.

"...And, watch them po-lice baby. I saw a bloody one in my dreams last night, and you were just a kicking and screaming at him. I know you working for the cause, but you have 4 children here who don't need their mama to be in jail." Passion was still nodding, but with her eyes closed. She tried not to squint when Mama Lettie told her about the cop; she had seen him too.

"Mama Lettie, I'm staying as far away from them pigs as I can."

"Well, you better, 'cause they don't treat the women folk no different from the men, they like to beat on everybody."

Mama Lettie whispered that last part, knowing better than to scare the children, but Mama Lettie couldn't control her concern, she loved her Passion; she had known Passion from the day she was born; she was actually the mid-wife who brought Passion into the world. She and Mattie, Passion's deceased mother, had a sisterhood similar to the one Passion shared with Anne and Connie. The two had come from the same home–Wilmington, North Carolina. They had left dreaming of big city living, then going back one day and buying land. "You ain't got nothing if you ain't got no land." Everybody knew that.

Neither Passion nor her children ever quite understood the depth of the love Mama Lettie felt for them, or what she saw when she looked at them with Mattie's eyes. Seeing them everyday made her think of Mattie everyday, keeping her alive. She often told the children stories of how they met in the train station in Wilmington, bound for New York and a new life. Lettie was 15 and very much ashamed then having left her first born, which would turn out to be her only child. Mattie, on the other hand, was an unwanted child being sent to live with a great aunt. She had been 14 and very afraid. The two decided to hold on to one another the moment they became friends, and vowed to never let the other go. No matter what. It was quite the coincidence that they were both bound for Brooklyn, if you believed in coincidences; and they didn't.

Within months, Mattie's great aunt died, leaving her homeless and without kin. Lettie had been working in a hospital, and once she had saved enough money, she had gotten her own flat. Her kin had not turned out to be the church folk she was told they were, and had no problem feeding one less person. Mattie and Lettie became roommates and soul sisters for life. The flat Mattie had found was in Browns' Village, near lots of homefolk, the Long Island Railroad and plenty of day work. Mattie went to work right away, and the soul sisters' life in the big city had begun.

Sam Cooke singing, "Darling...you...oo...oo...oooh...send me", brought Mama Lettie back to 1963, She was eyeing Passion's reaction to hearing Justice's favorite song, and quickly decided to change the subject.

"You children don't know how lucky you are to even get to go to school. Back when me and your Grandma was growing up, we had to work. Ain't that right Miss Passion?" Mama Lettie could see that Passion was still preparing for her departure and trying to ignore the song she used to love, "...that's all right, go'on girl, do what you got to do." She waved her hand at Passion like she was flagging down a taxicab.

"I'll be right with you Mama Lettie. You know I'm not leaving 'til we pray." She almost yelled as she ran into the back room to gather some literature she needed to hand out on the bus. The phone kept ringing too, but Tres had been prepped to relay all necessary messages. Mama Lettie just watched them all for a second. She saw Mattie in each one of those children. And Passion. Well, Passion looked so much like her mother, it sometimes made Lettie forget what year it was. She had Mattie's gestures and the silly smirk she used to wear when she wasn't comfortable. Seeing the usually composed Passion a little frantic while preparing for the onslaught, reminded her of the night in 1937 when she and Mattie rushed to Sister Jones' side. She held the youngest girl, Zaire and fought the old memory.

It had been Tuesday night, the night they had always had the Sisterhood gathering to prepare for baptism down at Canarsie Pier. Mattie and Young Reverend Franklin had become the perfect couple, and with the help of Sister Lettie, had started a strong, though small fellowship. Except, this night, the strong alto voice belonging to Sister Jones was sorely missed. "We gotta get Jones, Lettie, you know can't nobody take me to the water like Sister Jones", was the only laugh they'd have that night. Before they had even reached the small house, they could hear the painful moans from within. Sister Jones had given up on screaming when the pain tripled. She lay there in a pool of blood still gushing from between her legs. "He left me here to die," she whispered, "took my money and left me here to die." Mattie almost passed out at the gruesome sight. Lettie recalling the scene and the horror mouthed the words she spoke to Mattie that night. "Get my herb bag Mattie, hurry up girl, she's dying." Lettie tore rags, boiled them and packed Sister Jones up while Mattie was gone. She did all she could to keep the 20-year-old woman conscious: ice on her chest and eyes, unceasing prayer, she even told a few jokes just to make her speak. That's when he came back.

Mattie was down the street tripping over herself trying to remember what all herbs belonged in the empty bag. She had grabbed the valerian, and red raspberry for the bleeding, the hyssop, the catnip, and the primrose oil. Rev. Franklin couldn't get her attention and had decided to run after her as she ran out of the house and down the street. As God would have it, he had paced himself behind Mattie with just enough quick steps to witness the abortionist knock her down on his way out of the door. The flushed quack had had the audacity to return to the scene of the crime, threatening to "finish the job" if Sister Jones didn't give him more money. He had gotten 20, now he wanted $40 more. Reverend Franklin almost committed murder that night; some still believed he had because that was the last anyone had *ever seen of the butcher who always lurked in Browns' Village's darkness. The reverend's good buddy from the marines, then young, Joseph Justice, assisted him in rebuking the devil. Justice was known to be good at eliminating the enemy. Unfortunately, it was done all too late for Sister Jones.*

*Mama Lettie had a snarl on her face like Passion had never seen her wear. It was the terrifying anger any Negro wore when facing the diabolic hatred racism created. Reliving the Sister Jones episode took the edge off of Mama Lettie and helped her to reme*mber why Passion had to go to the front lines today. She looked at her differently now ... unafraid ... and faithful; she prayerfully claimed her victory and safe return.

"Don't worry 'bout the children, I'll make sure everyone gets where they need to go!"

"Thank-you Mama Lettie, you know I appreciate your loving support. I don't know what I did to deserve you. Looking down and hugging in big scoops, Passion grabbed each of her babies who were waiting her warmth, her comfort—the Mommy-feeling that says, "everything will be fine."

"Mama Lettie," Passion looked worried now, "you all right?" she asked softly. "Please don't worry, we'll be fine. The brothers are turning out in record numbers, and you know they're gonna do the do." They both laughed.

Lettie was still trying to come back to '63, "Just don't make me have to come down there to that school. Them crackers ain't ready to handle Ready Lettie." They were laughing hard and holding one another tightly. Lettie didn't wish to alarm Passion by holding her tighter, although her spirit begged her to; she knew Passion would not be the same when she'd return. At this point, the children were either hugging Passion or Lettie and moving towards their Mommy's lips and warmth.

"Just please remember: the boys need to be at the shop by about 8:30, the girls need to be at day camp by 9:00. I figured y'all could just walk down the block together at 8:40 or so. Papa Joe won't mind if they're a few minutes late." Passion could feel Tres looking at her and knew what he was about to say. "Don't worry Tres, you can make up your missed ten- minute shine tomorrow. Mommy wants y'all sticking close today."

"I wasn't even gonna say that Ma." He was smiling sarcastically. Then he kissed her face as Deuce had done earlier, before she headed to the door.

Mama Lettie stared into Passion's eyes. Worry and pride mixed with tears she wouldn't allow to fall. She closed her eyes and gave Passion a big mama's hug, but behind her eyelids the fire and the bloody cops waited for her. Lettie sighed deeply, and let Passion go.

"Mama loves you", she touched her face as they let go.

Passion yelled out brief reminders to them all and ended with, " ... and mind Mama Lettie, you may have dinner over there 'cause I don't know what time I'll be back." She stepped quickly down the corridor and down the front staircase. And, as soon as she did, the music stopped. Mama Lettie and the four children made a bee line straight across the hall, through Mama Lettie's Victorian-styled living room, and quickly positioned their heads and contorted their bodies to watch Passion and the masses of beautiful black people. They each tried to get the best angle from the three-part rectangular window. The girls had their faces plastered to the closed smaller window panes located at the bottom and were on either side of the boys, who had the middle two portions opened and available for them to yell their last good-byes to Passion, as she'd exit the building. Mama Lettie stood over them all. She felt sorry for the girls and allowed them to stand on the windowsill to see, then wave and yell to their Mama. This was something she had never done before; but this was a day she'd never seen. Folks had come from every kind of church: Episcopal, Pentecostal, Baptist, Catholic, Seventh Day Adventist, A.M.E.; they had all been inspired by the times, the voices of strength and by actions like the Montgomery Bus Boycott and the children of Little Rock, Arkansas. And, everyone looked good too. Black folk were protesting in style. Sunday best was in fierce competition with Easter suits and dresses. No one would dare wear a thing less than best on an honorable occasion as this. Fighting the "good fight" was always known as God's work. They went to war looking Christian, civilized and peaceful. And they were on one accord.

Ten yellow buses anxiously stood outside of The Browns' Village First Believers' Baptist Church. And, Reverend Mitchell, bullhorn in hand, stood on the top step proudly, showing all of his teeth. He was almost breathless at the sight of over 300 people gathered before him. He and the Parents for Equal Education Committee had only expected 100, with luck and prayer. But just last night, ministers from all over Brooklyn began calling. They had heard the call and they were coming. It was well known that the popular civil rights leader, Medgar Evers had just been killed, and brothers and sisters were tired of feeling powerless.

"We're gonna turn this thing around", each one had stated, in one-way or another before hanging up.

"Amen...AMEN! Brother" or "Sister." the reverend had replied each time. By the end of the last call Reverend Mitchell felt almost delirious. A feeling of euphoria welled up inside of him.

"God's gonna give us this school sister. We're going to make history tomorrow." He had told Passion 11:00 the night before. She couldn't help but be excited as well.

"Maybe this is what my life has been leading up to", she thought to herself, hanging up the phone, "...maybe this is my purpose".

Watching from her fourth floor window, Mama Lettie was overwhelmed by it all herself. Imagine so many colored people, gathered together. And that young Reverend Mitchell reminded her so much of Reverend Franklin; the reminiscing of 26 years before continued uncontrollably. Her senses were tingling still, and it wasn't just from the nightmares. Death was lingering in the air. She felt its grip coming and she knew it was close. She hurried the children along. Seeing Free, her old friend Joseph Justice (she called him "Free", short for his family name—Freeman), would make her feel better. She needed to see his face, to know if he was feeling what she was feeling.

Most of the buses were filled. Gray exhaust filled Sutter Avenue, although a few members of "First Believers'" had still not boarded. Passion sat with Anne and Connie in the first of the two buses containing "First Believers'" members. They sat anxiously, discussing how unbelievable it all was. They had planned this day back in May when the busing project was first brought to their attention. Passion, as usual, had no problem sending her children to a different neighborhood, especially if it meant they would get a better education. She was the one who helped Reverend Mitchell convince most people that it was a good idea. Then they found out that the Whitestone community was fighting against their school being integrated. They had even gone as far as threatening to burn the church. Some of the parents cowered in fear, resorting to enrollment at their notoriously deficient neighborhood school, but many seethed in anger, chanted "We shall not be moved!", and began to plan the protest.

"Here we go.", Passion whispered to herself, and the spirit riding with her.

By the time the buses pulled out it was almost 9:00. Passion's back window view showed Mama Lettie talking to Papa Joe in front of the Dew Drop Inn Record Shop. Both stopped to wave, which they had done a few hundred times already. The girls were in camp. Deuce and Tres had already begun shining shoes. They looked up and waved at the thought of their Mama's waving hand since they couldn't really see her. They knew she could see them and that she was waving too. Mama Lettie waved again and nodded right in Passion's direction. Her eyes fixed on them, Passion continued to see the picture of Mama Lettie standing over Deuce, an aura of light hovering over his afro and under Lettie's hand as her blue cotton dress hem blew in Tres' face. He attempted to wave while pushing it lightly. Papa Joe had his hand on Tres' head. They grew smaller–and smaller–and smaller; finally going out of sight as the bus ascended the hill that divided Browns' Village and East Village.

Her eyelashes, slightly intertwined, joined completely, and changed Passion's mental-television channel back to Justice. Toasted corn muffins, bagels and coffee being distributed battled his scent this time. Deuce looked more like him everyday, she thought. Deuce's face flashed before her, off and on like a neon sign. Deuce. Justice. Deuce. Justice.

Justice and the smell of what she always described as "the sensual sea water," filled her nostrils, her heart and her mind. It was actually Old Spice; like most groomed cosmopolitan "colored" men, including his father, Justice had worn it everyday. Some how it smelled differently on him. Simply alluring, it was to Passion.

She tried to come back, but it was difficult this time. She wondered if thinking of him so often made her overly possessive of his spirit–if there was any such thing. What if she was holding on to something that needed to be let go? It had been four years since he had been killed. That really isn't very long ago. "Give it time," she remembered Mama Lettie saying. "Time heals all wounds." It had before, when death had robbed her. But Justice's death was different; though just as unexpected as her parents' and brothers' deaths. Justice dying was somehow not final, not complete. Sometimes, it was as if he hadn't died at all. She couldn't see or hear him, but she felt him, and oh God, she smelled him so often, she often expected him to appear. She would feel all tingly when the sense was aroused; and every hair on her body would stand up and waver back and forth. Then, she would not be able to stop grinning, not smiling, but grinning like she had when she was 15 and caught him staring at her.

For thirteen years of her young life, Passion had loved Justice wholly: spiritually, brotherly, motherly, amorously and mutually. It was hard to stop now. Passion often dreamed of their past as she did now on the bus, en route to fulfilling one of her and Justice's dreams. From the time they realized they were expecting, both pledged to give their children college educations, to make them leaders, healers, emancipators of their race. This they had vowed for themselves as well.

Together, as teenagers, they had decided to live a clean, righteous and meaningful life. They would be the go-getters, the radicals–the ones to bring the revolution to Browns' Village. They had always planned to unite and educate the brothers and sisters in the community, which was a dream and responsibility passed on to them from Justice's father, Joseph Justice Freeman Sr., known to all as Papa Joe. "Colored" and "Nigger" were slowly dying at this time, and the American Black felt stronger than ever. A larger percentage of educated youth obviously possessed the spirits of their restless ancestors, just as Passion and Justice. She remembered their very first conversation, when had they discussed the poor conditions of most Negro communities, "How we needed to stand up and call ourselves black, and do something about this", his voice was in her ear.

Reverend Franklin, her dad, had preached one Sunday about "Putting on the whole armor of God" and being unafraid to fight for the good of your people. Reverend had taught about a "colored" man named Charles Houston, who fought in the World War—had won medals and done great things, risking his life for his country; and in return had felt the razor-sharp sting of racism. "This man had decided to use the U.S. Constitution against its hypocritical laws and law makers by fighting racism in the courtroom." They learned, that day, that amongst winning several court cases in the name of equality, Mr. Houston also produced the first team of black lawyers, amongst them the first black Supreme Court Justice—Thurgood Marshall.

Passion and Justice were in love with Houston and the idea of fighting the system, with the system. They spoke incessantly of the ingenious plan. Having knowledge of the law—Yes! Taking Uncle Sam to court—Yes! It sounded good to them. "Maybe we'll even get our forty acres and a mule," they had laughed but taken the seriousness to heart. They both knowingly possessed some uncanny, inseparable connection to their ancestors. They loved it but didn't quite understand why. The fight for reparations for over 20 million Africans lost in the Middle Passage, killed and violated every year thereafter, never left their thoughts.

Justice and Passion had one heart, locked in just that, justice and passion. This is why she still smelled him. Every time they had made love, from that very first night—under the boardwalk at Coney Island, Easter Sunday 1950, 'til the very last time—the morning before he was shot, his pores reeked of a scent that incited her fire. They wouldn't just mate, they poured their souls into one another and became one each time, loving purely, unashamedly and uninhibitedly. Passion was always completely receptive to Justice's incredulous sensual maturity, and she made it her job to escort him from ecstatic pleasure to ecstatic pleasure. They star-launched one another's spirit with tantalizing tongues until what appeared as divine light embraced their interlocked bodies. The thought, which appeared to Passion in a flash, overheated her as well, causing her to blush and peek peripherally to see if anyone on the bus had witnessed her sensual flashback. The oft-visited memory always left her bewildered and blown away at the non-existent stage of ignorant exploration between them. It had appeared as if their love-making was merely a continuation from their past lifetime. Even initially, behaving as if in a trance, each had been drawn to the other's erotic zones, liberating energy without any guidance. Undeniable enhancement had rewarded every touch, every thought—every time. *He filled her nostrils.* Her heart raced.

"Enough of this," she thought she actually had said aloud. She batted her eyes and stretched them wide to get a grip on reality. Passion crossed her legs and forced herself to focus on the on-coming battle.

"Busted!" Anne whispered in singing thought when she saw Passion mildly rubbing, and then clutching her neck, feeling for the onyx beads Justice had given her on the last Christmas they spent together. They seemed to massage her neck as he used to do, and she had a habit of feeling them subconsciously whenever she thought of him. She would eventually find herself clutching or rubbing them, look down at her hands as if they were operating on their own, and then push the beads back beneath her top. Passion felt eyes and decided they were most likely Anne's. That was cool. She un-twirled the beads and smiled in Anne's direction. Anne smiled too, and then glanced away. She knew what year it was for Passion and understood that Passion was probably fighting with her memory again. Anne looked back at Passion, then quickly caught the title on the passing marquis of the Sutter RKO Theatre, then she joined Passion on the back seat of the bus.

Above, an impatient crowd of Manhattan-bound Brownsvillians leaned over the three-story, iron rail and watched the yellow buses sputter down Sutter Avenue. They skeptically discussed and bet on the fate of the well-dressed warriors as they awaited the last rush hour train on the platform of the el train. They were well unaware that tonight, when they disembarked the 6:15 on the adjacent platform, life in Browns' Village will have changed forever. Some prayed. Some cried. Others shrugged their shoulders, unable to understand why anyone would even attempt to fight the devil. Sighing loudly, or just shaking their heads with syncopated staccato moaning, "umf, umf, umf," was repeated for a spell. While a few residents recalled tales of "back home" and the "klan," many resigned to thinking of the workday they were about to face. Trying not to sweat first thing in the morning, one group unconsciously drifted into the un-welcomed heat, prayed for a breeze and stared into the horizon. Floating with the approaching visible heat, they hovered over roof tops of stores and tenements, looked into opened windows, glided over the increasing traffic below and followed the yellow buses until the last one turned left onto Pennsylvania Avenue.

Ritually, neighborhood straphangers stood hypnotized by the view from the el's platform. Before boarding the train, they watched Pete the Barber offering a shine to passers-by. He was known as a jolly man, laughing and talking to everyone before entering the train station or the factory entrance, was his daily routine. It was difficult not to peer sorrowfully at the factory workers since the view from the platform led directly into the third floor window of the brand-less clothing manufacturing plant. They sewed for hours on end without a break or a minimum wage.

The elevated tracks shook. But, once the brownsvillians had embarked, a note of joy was heard down Sutter Ave. Defying the hot morning sun, Papa Joe had begun awakening the late sleepers with music that was universally loved–Motown.

"Everybody say YEAAH!" Little Stevie Wonder commanded joyfully
into the street.
"YEAH!
"Say YEAAH!"
"YEAAH!'
"...Yeah, Yeah, Yeah!, his harmonica continued, coercing everyone in
earshot into head bopping or doing the jerk.

Even if this was the fifth time this song was heard today, the music
Little Stevie created still had a way of paralyzing your thoughts and
motions–taking you on a ride through funky horn sections and back beats
that controlled your muscles. Although the heat was rising, no one seemed
to mind. The sky was a beautiful, cloudless, aqua blue, so the sun bathed
anyone who dared to venture out in it. But, no one seemed to mind as
they bopped passed the Dew Drop Inn. Papa Joe was giving everyone a little soul juice to take with them on the train. He knew they'd be humming
all they way to the city after drinking in some Stevie Wonder. The rush
hour ride was a job in itself, he knew, "might as well make it as pleasant as
possible"- especially on a hot day like today.
Tres and Deuce loved it best because they were lucky enough to work in
The Dew Drop Inn and hear great musicians like Little Stevie, Marvin
Gaye, Jackie Wilson and other soul greats of the early 60's. They had pru-
dently designated the front of the record shop as their shoeshine pit stop.
Papa Joe had given them permission to rent out the space as long as they
promised to "Shine those shoes so well that folks'll come inside and buy a
record." He wasn't only their boss, but he was the their grandfather, and the
only black proprietor on Sutter Avenue. He was also an esteemed elder in
the community; everyone respected Papa Joe. He had been a good father to
Justice and had prayed that his name would be a prelude to a reality for his
people. Papa Joe had never expected things to turn out this way.

He and Justice had trained an army of brothers. The ones Uncle Sam hadn't recaptured and sent to die in the jungle, were now getting caught up in this new drug thing–shooting smack in your veins. Many of the ones who made it back had returned as junkies–addicted to junk. Justice knew who was behind it all, but they shot him down before he could get the information back to Papa Joe. Now Justice was dead and all Papa Joe could do to keep sane was to keep the spirit of Justice alive in Tres and Deuce, and, keep his soldiers on the front line. There were still a few soldiers on the scene; they were well trained and could now train younger brothers. But the main two recruits-to-be were Tres and Deuce. All eyes were on them at all times. They had to be protected.

Tres and Deuce couldn't be happier. All they knew was they were earning their own money, listening to the best music in the world all day, and hanging out with their grandfather. They considered themselves the luckiest 11 and 12-year-old boys on the block–so did the other boys. Papa Joe had even refused to accept the percentage of their pay Mama told them to offer. He knew that the boys were using the money to help out the family and was really using the opportunity to get to know his grandsons better, and of course, teach them what their dad would have if he were still alive. He grasped every chance he got to teach them lessons in responsibility, finances and how to be a man. But, most importantly, to the boys, he taught them about music–the greatest music they could ever want to hear. He had become more like a friend than a grandfather to them, though his appearance bore the epitome of eldership. He looked like grandfather of all grandfathers with his gray and white afro and long, matching beard when he strolled through "the village" balancing rhythmically with his exquisitely, hand-carved African walking stick.

The boys felt comfortable and secure with Papa Joe, even though they had never been this close to him before. Just six months ago, he was not more than an old man Mama always made them kiss and hug whenever they passed the record shop. He'd always give each of them a dime with a lady on it–the girls especially loved that part. Then he'd rub the boys' heads and say how much they looked like their daddy when he was their ages. He had spent some time with them before Justice was killed, but not this intensely. He was always so busy protecting the village; he barely had time to spend with his grands. He spent time with Justice, and sometimes came to Sunday dinner, but he hadn't taken them to the park since they were 5 and 6 years old—and they didn't even remember that. He changed after the funeral though. He had promised Justice, before he closed his eyes forever, that he'd raise his boys. Ages 11 and 12 were prime ages to begin their "warrior training," Papa Joe had told them. Deuce and Tres had looked at one another with perplexed grins, wanting to laugh, but knowing better. They didn't know what "warrior training" was, but they were game. It was set to begin at the beginning of the summer. Their special reward would be a trip to the World's Fair in Queens. While at the shop, they asked Papa Joe all sorts of questions. Things they couldn't ask Mama. And Papa Joe explained everything from puberty to marriage, despite Tres' insistence that he already knew it all. Papa Joe even explained the importance of a proper diet. He had just learned of the dangers of meat, poultry and fish himself and wanted to ease the boys into vegetarianism. He had warned them not to eat school lunch, "to get off that beef and stop drinking milk." Passion had never given them pork, so that lecture wasn't necessary. In time they would look like mini replicas of Papa Joe. They had both already started wearing Afros—though their's were short for the time being. Papa Joe had also explained the strength one had in his hair. Most of the time they dressed alike, wearing their African print dashikis and dungarees—just like Papa Joe. Although most people dressed in common western clothing, the boys loved being different. But, most of all, they loved looking like Papa Joe.

The boys had begun a daily routine of working until 10, then going for fountain sodas from the drug store next door. It was owned by old Mr. Bernstein. He was grumpy most of the time, but the boys knew he liked them. His bleach-blonde wife and teen-aged daughter worked at the store also. They were always smiling and talking about "what the neighborhood was like years ago, when we first moved here." Freddy's Toy Store was also a pit stop on the home from time to time. Passion would rarely allow the purchasing of comic books, but they could sometimes talk her into it. The green and yellow old-fashioned luncheonette on the corner still sold hamburgers 2 for 25 cents. The boys thought that was a great bargain though Mama Lettie often told stories of buying a whole dinner for 10 cents and getting on the train for a nickel.

The neighborhood was a comfortable and safe home for Tres and Deuce though an obvious transition had begun. Many residents were now predominately "colored," contrasting the remaining storeowners who lived outside of Browns' Village. All except Hannah Williams and Papa Joe, who wisely invested in the storefront when he retired from the Marines. Nonetheless, everyone knew one another and looked out for each other. And, everybody knew Tres and Deuce. The two used to sweep in front of Pete's Barber Shop for a few extra bucks during the winter, then decided a shoeshine business would be a more lucrative endeavor.

Sutter Avenue, where they were known as the Freeman Brothers, belonged to Tres and Deuce. They were only "Tres" and "Deuce" to their family and close friends though. "Tres, because his name was Joseph Justice Freeman the third, and "Deuce" because he was the second son. When they weren't playing on Sutter Ave, they were working on Sutter Ave. The building they lived in was on Sutter Ave. It was constructed with a basketball court right in front, which incidentally had their names carved on it. Their bedroom window even faced Sutter Ave. So, from their fourth floor window, they could see all the action. As they looked down the tree-lined block their development was on, they could even see The Dew Drop Inn. In the evenings, they would watch for Passion to walk down from the Sutter Avenue station. Deuce was usually the look out who would warn the others as soon as he's see her graceful gait to "finish cleaning up 'cause Mama's COMIN'!!!"

The boys had taken Papa Joe's advice and generosity to heart and had lined up a string of regular customers, generating enough cash to bring money home to Passion and still buy a new Motown 45 every week at a "workers' discount". The older men enjoyed having their shoes shined at The Dew Drop Inn partially because the name itself reminded them of home. Trees in the south always dripped with dew in the early morning. When the sun shone on the dew, "it was like God was kissing you Good Morning," they often retold. They also loved the way the boys "spit-shined like they used to back in the service." Papa Joe had taught them well. He would entertain the elders with his special jazz segment, which began promptly at 10:15—Papa Joe's favorite time of the day. The boys would have returned from their soda break, and it was "Jazz n Shine Time." Smiling old brown men gladly sat in comfortable, old kitchen chairs as they tapped their feet to the likes of Charlie "Bird" Parker, Lester Young, Duke Ellington, Horace Silver, Dexter Gordon, King Pleasure, Dizzy Gillespie, and every other jazz master Papa Joe could use to ignite his stereo unit and watch the old men become young again. Shaking their heads, they made statements like: "Man, you hear that riff?" and then tried to out-scat one another.

This was the part of the day when Sutter Avenue had magic. The spirit was different from when the Rhythm n Blues played, or even on Sunday mornings when Gospel reigned and people sometimes stopped and shouted right there on the street. People got lost in the Jazz; and it captured anyone passing by. Syncopated rhythms followed men and women to work, fastening to dress and jacket hems. Ella Fitzgerald's high pitched "Skip-skip-skip-a-did-a-diddle" went up the street, passed the drug store, the toy store, the luncheonette; turned the corner, faced the barber shop, then mounted the steps to the Manhattan-bound el. Pete the Barber missed his workers; he had tried to convince them to bring their shoeshine business to the barbershop.

"Lots of business right here near the train station boys, you can catch folks on their way up the stairs."

"No thank-you Mr. Pete," they had declined with each invitation. Pete made working for him sound like a lifetime in Paradise. He'd cunningly whisper to the boys whenever they passed with his eyebrows raised, looking slyly from side to side, as if the information was top secret. This cracked the boys up. "We're working for our Papa Joe," they'd remind him. He knew just as well as they did that people passed his barber shop near the train everyday on their way to The Dew Drop Inn for the shine that you can sing and tap your free foot to. Mr. Pete could only smile and agree with everyone who knew that Passion Freeman sure had her two good boys, "...and they were well mannered too".

It was well passed eleven when the morning rush was finally over. As usual for that time of day, the two, still clean boys sat, crouched down behind a counter inside the record store counting their wages. The same boys usually so entranced with the music singing to them from the speakers were now oblivious to all but their jingling coins an stiff bills. The two were a beautiful sight to the old man who loved to listen to the loving exchange between the brothers and witness how well-trained and dignified the young boys were, right down to their shapely cut 'fro's. They were of similar build, though the younger one, Deuce, was slightly taller than his brother Tres. But no one would ever know it to listen to them "rap". Deuce had the utmost respect for his older brother, who loved him dearly and advised him on every aspect of his young life with wisdom some adults never attain. Deuce had the Freeman physique, but Tres had his parents' wisdom and strength. Memories of conversations about music, politics and "the struggle" between him and his own brother came back to old Joe as he watched the boys. The youthful chatter then broke his stare and spell.

"Man, by September, we're gonna be rich Tres."

"I don't know about rich Deuce, but we'll have enough to buy our school clothes at the end of the summer, and maybe a record player. We could even help Mama by buying Zaire and Mecca's clothes."

"Look at this!, Man we are rich!"

"We're not rich Deuce, won't you be cool." Papa Joe was laughing, pretending he wasn't listening. "I wish we would've thought of this last year, we could have got those new Pro Keds like Eddie has."

"Yup, but that's all right Tres, 'cause we can sure get 'em now." Both boys vow, as they promised, to take care of family business first. Tres is the most serious about his position and constantly reminds Deuce that they owe it to their late father to take care of the family. He even rubs his younger brother's head as his father used to when he agrees to "present Mama with all of the money to surprise her instead of buying a record player. Well—maybe not every dime," they nodded and laughed.

"Time for you two to break for lunch, your Mama's supposed to call and check on you while you're home." Papa Joe's voice startled Deuce, causing him drop the stacks of quarters he was rolling.

"Mama said we could get hamburgers from the luncheonette Papa," Tres wanted to remind Pap Joe, knowing how he feels about meat.

"Go on then, but this'll be your last. Your Mama and I will talk about that tomorrow. Hurry up now. I don't want her to worry none."

The boys quickly finished rolling up their coins and stuffed them in their pockets. They slapped Papa Joe five and started preparing to race to the corner. Papa Joe stroked his gray and black beard, as he had a habit of doing when he was anticipating something. He straightened out his orange and black African print dashiki by flattening it against his broad chest and thick sides before he walked outside to greet three tall brothers wearing dark shades and Afros. They always met with Papa Joe around this time of day.

"You forgot your ball boys," he yelled as he met the brothers with a complicated handshake Deuce and Tres couldn't duplicate just yet. Tres smiled at the tall Afros who slapped him five as they passed. Deuce ran right into the one with the biggest 'fro; he was just born clumsy. He was a little scared at first, but the big brother only laughed at the mini replica of his lost friend Justice, picked Deuce up, then planted him on the ground. Deuce ran down the block, easily catching Tres, who took the head start.

"We'll get it on our way back Papa Joe." The boys had to pass the record shop on their way home. Right now they had burgers on the brain. All they had to spend was 75 cents for the 4 burger-2 soda meal. They planned to get their sodas from the drug store where bottles of Hammer bottled sodas were plenty and available in every flavor.

The boys stopped to check out the new DC comic books first, but Mr. Bernstein was even less pleasant than usual. The boys tried to smile and crack jokes to get him to laugh, but he continued to look stern and complained to them about how their grandfather and his friends were being too noisy today. Deuce and Tres shrugged their shoulders and proceeded out of the store. Deuce decided to go back for the basketball now so they could take the route through the projects after they got the girls, to see if Eddie was home. Tres agreed and continued across the street towards P.S. 63, where summer day camp was held. Deuce felt he shouldn't attempt to re-enter the record shop when he heard an argument, but he then became very concerned for his Papa Joe. The door flew open. He saw the angry cop. The gun—it was aimed right at his heart. He heard Papa Joe holler, but he couldn't move. The blast was so close it lifted the eleven year old into the air before he landed face up on the pavement outside The Dew Drop Inn.

Crowds were created within seconds of the resounding shot. Afros grabbed the cop and had him hemmed up in the corner of the Dew Drop Inn. Papa Joe was outside on his knees—holding Deuce. He actually saved the cop's life when he picked him up and literally threw him back into the record shop. Eliminating the pig is what Papa Joe actually had in mind, but he ended up stopping the furious crowd from seizing the officer and taking a life for a life. He couldn't allow anyone to die in prison for him or his family, even though the Browns' Village community was also his family. Especially poor Miss Lucy. She had seen it all. Her screams heightened at the sight of the angry officer unsteadily holding his revolver yelling, "I

SAID STOP NIGGER!!!" at the fleeing Afro. Blasting towards his back, he missed the skilled target, but hit Deuce's chest. It was enough to cause her to begin drinking again. She shook violently and continued to holler all the way back under the el, to Big Hip Hannah's place. A few women escorted her, crying with her all the way, unable to calm themselves enough to calm her down.

"REVOLUTION"—"STILL WATERS"

We screamed and we shouted
but never ever doubted
the power of our God
aiding to complete this awesome job

Protesting in peace
Protesting in pain
Nothing to lose
Everything to gain

Marching made courtrooms
out of blood-stained streets
Freedom songs saved souls
through wining waterhoses
and running, rhythmic feet

landing against segregated lunchroom counters
So picket sign-less, equality seekers surmounted
in broken silence
Wading in the still waters,
refusing to take the white man's orders

Protesting in peace
Protesting in pain
Nothing to lose
Everything to gain

Fed up with forced mis-education
Determined to insist on integration
Medgar Evers in mind
Martin King in sight
the spirit of Malcolm inspired the fight

Protesting in peace
Giving back the least
Passion opens the path,
welcoming the deadly aftermath.

C. Wright-Lewis 6/97

Chapter Three

▼

"Revolution"

WHITESTONE
Brooklyn, New York
(Three miles north of Browns' Village)
July 17, 1963
9:20 A.M.

The heat had reached the point that one could swim in its visible waves. Clad in only their sweaty skin and shorts, three brothers hovered over a deserted street corner, hanging in the visibly pulsating airwaves, and praying for the breath of fresh air they had left home to get. A white Cadillac–disguised as a potential breeze–waded towards them and created a gust that didn't make a damn difference. Martha and the Vandellas seeped through though,

"It's like a HEAT WAAAVE, burning in my heart, I can't keep from *CRY–YIN'*- it's tearing me A–part. YEAH! YEAH! YEAH! YEAH!"

The disc jockey broke in, ticking off the true fans. The controlled baritone commanded his audience, knowing he had what they wanted–the weather report. "It's 92 and it's still an hour before noon ... 102 with the heat index..." his voice was then faint. They stretched their heads for the last fading words as the hog sailed beach-ward in the waves. The boys smiled and held their arms up as long as they could, waving back at the kids in the back seat. The bright orange and yellow bathing suits waved again, struggling to turn around through the beach balls, coolers, picnic baskets and huge umbrellas.

Without discussion all three fought the desire to chase the white car and float into the fresh ocean air, instead, they sighed, then drifted towards home and an air of dissension that beckoned from down Arlington Avenue. Rarely heard raucous filled the heavy air. Augmenting, the sound fed them needed adrenalin then led them around the corner, one block down, and across the street, to the front of Whitestone Elementary School.

The hot, slight summer breeze offered a tinge of relief to the bared legs of the on-lookers, but not a gasp-full to the brothers who had had the nerve to work up a sweat. They all stood there looking puzzled and breathing hard like escaped asthmatics on a mission for air, but unable to resist the heated performance which promised to soon explode. Unmoved by the intensifying sun rays and lack of oxygen, the slave master's grandchildren marched. For hearts filled with white, American, law-making power and pride, they mustered up little noise with their little bullhorn. Listening unresponsively to the titmouse of a leader squeaking into the bullhorn, they marched slowly before the locked front door, not yet brave enough to dramatically display their slanderous beliefs on inequality though they had risen at dawn to rally against the intrusion of their white world.

Waving their American flags and picket signs pumped little blood into their weak heart. Herzog frowned in shame and shook his head. "Weak. Scared and weak." He grabbed the bullhorn and began to preach.

"You sound like you're not proud to be white! It's your right to protect what's yours. This is your school! This is your country! Our forefathers built this beautiful country with their bare hands! Why should you give up your birthright? What has been legally yours all your life is what you should keep! They only want to come here because they are not capable of teaching their own children. White teachers should teach white children and Nigger teachers should continue ruining theirs! Segregation NOW! Don't let niggers steal your child's education!"

This was all the cowards needed. He had lit their fuse. Ironically, his present followers and employers once hated the store-bought leader. For the last twenty years, they had referred to him as "vulgar", "barbaric" and "unnerving" due to his popular Aryan exploits and his uncanny resemblance to Adolph Hitler. But now they hung on his every word because they feared Black people and integration more than Nazis and white supremacy. They used their shame as their shield, but without his respect. He saw them as cowards. Edgar J. Herzog would stop the niggers all by himself if he had to; his followers couldn't be counted on anyway; they were still afraid to admit that they just like him and had always been. And as long as he was around, no one had to worry about any niggers going to school in Whitestone this or any other Fall.

"DON'T LET NIGGERS STEAL YOUR CHILD'S EDUCATION, WE NEED WHITE POWER FOR OUR ARYAN NATION!" he screamed into the snatched bullhorn. His screeching voice caused the bullhorn to make a piercing ring each time the madman bellowed, but Herzog was just getting started. Neither did it annoy the demonstrators.

Oddly, the irritating sound had an adverse effect on the white marchers, giving them a needed edge. They began to chime in, in an offbeat rhythm, "DON'T LET NIGGERS STEAL YOUR CHILD'S EDUCATION ... IT CAN HURT THE NATION! DON'T LET NIGGERS STEAL YOUR CHILD'S EDUCATION! DON'T LET..." it began to rise as each fearsome protestor fed off from another's courage to speak the ugly words. Like a crescendo, it reached its peak, but in an unmelodious pitch just as the buses filled with their enemies slowly pulled up right in front of them. The brothers watching from across the street were now joined by a large group of supporters who would not dare join, but wouldn't miss this exhibit of white unity. It was just as good as watching the klan parade on the streets of Birmingham.

Passion, Anne and Connie's faces were obviously suppressing anger. For the very first time, they gazed upon the segregated battlefield—Whitestone Elementary School. In its three short miles away from Browns' Village, reading and math scores were higher here, children learned French, Spanish and Italian; gymnastics and tennis were part of the physical education curriculum, books were plentiful, chairs and desks were not broken and children weren't forced to bring their own lunches because the cafeteria had been closed down by the Board of Health. And, parents weren't fed up to the point where they'd risk their lives, and the lives of their children to receive what every other American received without question or hesitation. Passive Resistance had arrived and was prepared to knock the white out of Whitestone—forever.

Passion, over-zealous as she could sometimes get, was the first to jump off of the bus. The white faces, mostly out of fear, bonded into one steel nerve and greeted her with,

"GO HOME NIGGERS, GO HOME!" and their offbeat, "DON'T LET NIGGERS STEAL YOUR CHILD'S EDUCATION!"

They were practically beating her in the head with their wicked words. Anyone a block away could have seen Passion's face change. Her round doe eyes became slithers and merged with her thick eyebrows as they lowered into her face. Her nostrils widened. Her breathing became deep and low. And a red-toned fury illuminated her brown face. Little did they know, Passion was a black Herzog—she was as extremist as he was when it came down to her rights and her people. She would have gladly fought the war alone if necessary, a lone picket sign, marching daily and slugging it out with Herzog one-on-one, if necessary.

"Justice!" then she yelled it, "JUSTICE!" Her right arm had thrust her fist erect as a militant, simultaneously with the word so the gesture seemed to force "Justice!" out of her mouth. But she then felt Reverend Mitchell's arm reach around her chest and pull her backwards. He knew Passion well and was well aware that justice meant more than equality to her. He whispered,

"Remember that we're all here. Don't worry Sister, we will get what we came for; God has already seen to that."

Passion raised her hands in the air palms up, and gestured that she was all right, but stood boldly, stared the whites in the whites of their eyes as she waited for her 299 back up units to disembark. The Whitestone residents stood silently in shock. The crescendo then built new strength and rose again, motivated by the fear of being out-numbered in one's own backyard. Yet, the chanting stuttered, stumbled, then all together lost its offbeat rhythm upon the sight of the 300 brown faces that stood before them.

The blacks sandwiched the open-mouthed bigots like an Oreo cookie, and forced them to listen.

"Bring the children out!" Reverend Mitchell had commanded right before as many as fifty children were led out of the last bus, through the outer layer of black bodies, into the middle of white bodies and right in front of Herzog and the other Whitestone leaders—the core of the chaos. This was the reverend's secret weapon. He had honestly believed in his heart that if the discriminating faculty and staff had to face the children, they wouldn't be able to stick to their decision.

"Children, these are your new teachers and school administrators—and some of these people are the parents of your future classmates. We wanted you to be formally introduced to the people who are descendants of those who enslaved our great-grand parents, yet children, they will not enslave you, nor will they take away your right to a good education. Your fore-fathers already paid the price for that!"

He was eloquent—stirring—but most of the whites weren't moved. He could see that and he began to get angry.

"And you teachers—hiding behind your picket signs, put them down. PUT THEM DOWN I SAY! Drop the signs and come and look at these sweet black, angelic faces."

Some of them did peek from behind their signs at the children. But they still showed no emotion or sign that they were about to change their minds. The children, dressed in their Sunday best, were very much afraid and were too small to see anything but legs and hear angry voices. As they looked up, it appeared as if the sky had closed in, so they stood together as closely as possible, held hands and listened closely for the reverend's usu-ally soothing voice. But it had changed.

Reverend Mitchell was standing so close to Herzog they could hear one another breathe. Herzog, completely unaffected by what he considered the reverend's "nigger preacher tricks", as he explained to his followers as a new coon tactic before, grabbed the bullhorn and began chanting loudly right in Reverend Mitchell's face.

"DON'T GIVE NIGGERS YOUR CHILD'S EDUCATION! WE NEED WHITE POWER FOR OUR ARYAN NATION!" but it sounded frantic and lonely.

Herzog hadn't realized that his protest song had become an aria. The yelling and that piercing ring from the bullhorn were beginning to rattle his people's nerves. And worse, it was scaring the children. They had all begun to shrink in fear. Some held hands and hugged each other. Between the heat of hate and the heat index, the Oreo cookie had begun to bake. The whites were beginning to tighten with fear, knowing they were surrounded. They really wanted to quit, but couldn't control Herzog. They could feel the rage of the blacks—the stares from their glares—their rising pulse. Their deep inhalations moved together causing the group to heave, as would a chest attempting to suck in all the air it had lost after during a foot race. Suddenly, as the mercury reached its peak, in the extremely intense moment of silence that always comes before the storm, a screaming police siren jarred the entire group. And, before anyone could exhale, the scene was infiltrated with a sea of blue uniforms, swinging Billy clubs and brandishing guns quickly surrounded the mass of blacks who appeared to have imprisoned the whites, who held the children captive, who encircled Herzog and Reverend Mitchell, who calmly raised his bullhorn to speak but lost control of his emotions.

"Officers we have children here!" his voice was cracking, "We are not violent—and our children are with us! If an officer harms a child today, I cannot promise that we will all remain peaceful! Please just allow them to get back on the bus. DO NOT HARM OUR CHILDREN!"

Passion knew he could not go on. Just the thought of losing someone's child after they had entrusted him with the precious life was too much for the reverend to handle.

"All we are here for is to get our children an equal education; now that's the law!" she spoke calmly as possible into the bullhorn, but the blacks began to chant,

"EQUAL EDUCATION! EQUAL EDUCATION! Remembering their anger, unafraid of the police they've known to be enemies of their community.

"Well, what about our kids?" yelled a red-faced mother, which gave needed incentive to Herzog, who began his Aryan chant all over again

"DON'T GIVE NIGGERS YOUR CHILD'S EDUCATION! WE NEED..."

"EQUAL EDUCATION! EQUAL EDUCATION!"

Suddenly inclined to stop, Passion felt the lines in her forehead separate as her eyes widened. It was as if she was warned to duck as everyone else in the crowd sucked in a giant inhalation. The entire visions of the next few minutes were given to her during the huge gasp. Passion witnessed heads being bashed in, shots being fired and heard the horrifying cries of the children. Her dream briefly came to mind. Breaking her spell of suspended animation, Passion screamed, "RUUUN!' as she physically began to push children in the direction of the school bus. Commands of the police, screams of women and children and the roars of men quickly filled the air as shots were fired, tear gas was released and nightsticks were wielded. Passion, a few alert parents, along with Reverend Mitchell and the revolutionaries collectively dropped and crawled through and around black and white legs towards the first bus.

The children watched frantically from the bottoms of bus windows, shaking as their parents and teachers traded punches and kicks; possessed, contorted faces hurled insults and dirty names back and forth. Some children covered their ears, forcing out the howling of evil that filled the bus from outside in. Still others just whimpered loudly, their tiny shoulders uncontrollably jerking up and down, and their tears streaming down shamelessly.

Passion found herself outside of the bus again dodging spinning Billy clubs, grabbing every black arm she could get a hold of and forcing them downwards through the tunnel of legs she plowed, pushing them all back to the bus. She herself only narrowly escaped the white, out-stretched backhand of the cop in front of her as she yanked Anne's light blue blouse to stop it from going in the wrong direction. The officer's attention was away from them so she didn't want to have to yell. Anne had gotten tangled between a 6 ft 2, red-haired, red-faced, overweight cop and one of the brothers–David Walker–who was taller, obviously stronger and a much darker red than the shaking, itchy- fingered blue pig who had been holding Anne, but was then forced to let her go. David was fearless. He had just come home from Hell. The smell of Viet Nam was still in his pores, in his clothes, in his mind. He couldn't wash it off; he couldn't wash it out, despite how much gin he drank at night. He continued to see the tropical trees and rice paddies, and in the back of his mouth, despite how much gin he drank, he still tasted vomit induced by the chemical napalm that was used on the yellow man and sent home in the black man in the form of a disease called Agent Orange. He still heard gunfire in the deepest still of the night where the quiet and the dark reigned, where he seldom slept.

The cookie image had become a crumbled mixture and then vanished. People had run quicker than a jungle stampede at the warning of incoming, voracious lions. The settled dust revealed the red-haired, red-faced cop and David entangled. David had the cop in a full nelson at this point, but the cop still would not drop the gun.

"David's gonna kill that cop! Y'all know David's gonna kill that cop!" Anne was screaming. Like her friend Passion, in emotional situations, she lost her cool completely. She had once seen a man shot in the head and couldn't find her voice for a week. She had always faulted herself for the killer not being found, and secretly feared he'd one day come after her. She had vowed since that time, not to ever go back into shock again in life–no matter what the situation. She now screamed at, and practically about, anything done out of the ordinary. So when Passion heard Anne's fear-filled scream, she knew it was seeing death. She knew she had to do something. So she found Herzog.

"I'll kill you nigger!–I'll *kill* you!"

Like an army tank, Herzog and Passion were rolling atop bodies: black, white, and blue. Bigots, revolutionaries and pigs jumped in and created a multi-colored snowballing mound which consumed everyone in its way, including David and the cop, and enabled many of the hand-cuffed and being- hand–cuffed protestors to break free. They hauled ass down lily-white Linwood Avenue and David Walker was in the lead.

The cops had wanted to arrest Passion, of course, thinking she had attacked Herzog, the Hitler clone, but he had hit her first.

"Yes I would like to press charges," she guffawed as she repeated her story to everyone on the bus. What she had so innocently left out of the story was how she had provoked the Hitler clone into hitting her when she had spotted him hiding under a Dodge, avoiding the white's paddy wagon line.

"Your honky ass is busted," she recalled saying as she envisioned his surprised face in her head. The look on his face, and the sight of him fighting the cops like a wild boar when they were hoisting him into the wagon was worth the black eye she was merited in the fight. He had attacked her like a barbaric cave man wrestling for meat, and she had tried her best to kick his honky-ass. Confronting the enemy face-to-face didn't put any fear in her heart; Passion loved combat. Hell–snipers and spies she despised. She was just glad everyone was safe and that David got away. She dug that brother; he was sure worthy of his name.

The police and their few captives had coughed simultaneously, their exhaust-filled lungs exhausted them as they beat their chests and watched the yellow buses filled with the infiltrators, each holding a round-trip ticket, successfully escape. Hidden neighborhood bystanders began to uncover, recover then walked deliberately home. They tried to shake off the experience and allow the sun's heat to thaw their frozen hearts. Holding on to the past, Herzog's insanity still filled the air, reviving the hatred. He began yelling from the wagon. The three brothers, along with the other residents yelled in his defense, then joined their handcuffed leader.

"White Power!" angrier, "WHITE POWER!!!–DON'T LET NIG-
GERRRSSS…"

"Listen to that fool–he's screaming like the devil." The blacks could
hear him as they exited the Whitestone vicinity in their yellow get-a-way
buses.

"Well what do you think he is Connie? We're all God's creatures; some
good, others are evil. Hell, he may not even be human."

Passion always said something that made Connie say to herself,
"What?" then she'd catch on later–much later. She looked at Passion
thinking, *"What?"*

The whole bus was quiet. Looking back. They had all just realized that
they had gotten away with their lives. We beat the paddy rollers again. We
out-slicked ole massa again, they all seemed to be thinking. All except
Connie, who still had a puzzled look on her face. One could tell she was
still asking herself if Passion meant white people ain't really human or…?
She was thinking too hard as usual. Since Connie had only been in the
states from Panama about 18 months, there was a lot she didn't know. She
loved and trusted Passion's spirit from the moment they had met and
always listened to her advice. They had met in the Laundromat and discovered their children were the same ages. That's when Passion began to school
Connie about racism in the school system, in the cities, in the country and
in the world. Connie never realized that it was so broad. She had thought
that only the Africans in Panama caught Hell. Anne had felt the same way.
She was from Jamaica and thought "Yankee" life was better than life in
Jamaica. After meeting Passion, she was a little more politically conscious
too, and she had been in the states for ten years. She had to admit, Passion
taught History better than any teacher she had ever had in school.

Passion could see that Connie had that naive look on her face again and
smiled to herself, shaking her head. She looked back at the sleeping children in the back of the bus and pictured her two handsome boys and two
doll-faced beautiful daughters. She then felt a chill in the midst of heat.

Although Passion always appeared to be confident, in control, and conscious of all that was going on around her, she was never completely comfortable. She was well aware of every organism in her immediate
environment, not because of her innate warrior instinct, but because she
was afraid of being caught off-guard–being taken by someone "laying in
the cut". After all, that is how they got Justice, her Mama and her Papa.
None of them even knew what hit them when they were killed; especially
Mama and Papa who had been murdered in cold blood by a crazed junkie
with a homicidal "jones." Mama and Papa had known this young boy and
had watched him grow and had watched him deteriorate–transforming
into a ceaselessly scratching, head nodding zombie. His name was simply–"Brother"–that's what everyone called him. And before somebody took
him to "cloud nine", he had been everybody's brother. Selling newspapers,
especially on Sunday, was what he was known for, besides being a junior
usher at the church. As a delivery boy, he had been in everyone's home.
This is why Brother had found it very easy to rip people off. No one suspected him initially, "You know you can trust Brother," was what they used
to say. After he was busted in the staircase shooting up, the word was out,

"Don't trust *that* brother!"
But, some non-believers refused to accept the truth,
"I've known Brother all his life, he's like my own son."
"All that boy needs is some love–he'll come around."

They'd nod and agree. Passion's Mama and Papa were amongst the non-
believers, but of course they had never witnessed the wrath of the demonic
drug heroin, nor observed the metamorphosis of a saint into a possessed
specter who had traded everlasting life for everlasting death. They wore a
look of shock upon their wide-eyed and open-mouth faces when they
were found dead in the large frequently visited apartment.

Everyone had known that Brother was the culprit. Passion's two elder brothers had discussed their plan with her and their two youngest brothers after the funeral.

"To Hell with the cops!", she had remembered them saying,

"We'll pick Brother's junkie ass up from that new drug crib we saw him going in last night. He's been hiding out there for the last 3 days, but his ass is grass now!"

"Don't worry y'all, we still have each other," had been her contribution. Then they all hugged; Passion could still feel that too.

But instead of that feeling being comforting to her, it caused paranoia to emerge. She now felt as alone as she had 15 years ago when they all left her—one at a time. Because of the way it had all gone down, she felt that either she was cursed—or that she was destined for greater things than she could ever want or imagine—and it better had been the latter. But it was all beginning to wear her out. Sometimes she'd think of Justice but no scent or sense of him would enter her. And she just felt hollow inside. Passion hated that. On a bad day like that, not even the children could help her shake it. Today, on the other hand, she had felt him strongly, and everybody else too. She thought of her two older brothers—Hannibal and Musa who had both died in Viet Nam two years after Mama and Papa. They had been talked into joining the service after they had missed the hit on Brother. Then, her younger brothers, Big Man and Little Ray had been sent to live with North Carolina relatives and she hadn't been able to find them since. After several trips and phone calls to various friends and kinfolk, she could only pray they were still alive. She remembered their faces when she had last seen them so many years ago, waving good-bye to her from the Greyhound Bus at Port Authority Bus Station. Whenever she fought for children, she was fighting for them as well as her own. Because it had always been her responsibility to care for them when their parents were alive, she felt very of guilty that they were not in her care now. She vowed to her dead parents that she'd get them back after relatives had left with them, but she was only fourteen herself, and

under the care of Mama Lettie, who along with spiritual intervention, finally
got Passion to realize that God was not punishing her.

The more she lost of her immediate roots, the more Passion searched
for and identified with her ancestral roots. Maurya, her great-great grandmother often called out to her in the middle of the night. This would
happen often back when Passion was a child. But once her parents were
killed, Maurya began to appear to her. On each and every occasion,
Passion would be awakened at three o'clock in the morning by the sound
of sweet, melodious humming. She'd feel a light imprint at the head of her
bed and the soft stroking of the hair on her head. The first time this happened, Passion had been up crying all night. She had been so distraught
that she didn't even feel the stroking when it started. The next thing she
knew, she had fallen asleep. Amazed at the comfort that she felt from the
supernatural presence, Passion immediately assumed her mother had
descended from heaven to ease her mourning heart.

The next morning she had felt as content as a well-nursed baby. What
followed would be a resurgence of energy and stability, which would help
her through her present crisis. Each time she had lost a piece of her heart
through death, and felt she could not go on, the spirit would come. And,
each time she would be comforted, reaffirmed and recommitted to her
cause. It was Maurya, her personal comforter, who gave her life over and
over again, who with every stroke of the head was reconnecting Passion
with her African heritage. Though the spirit never spoke, Passion believed
she had received messages from looking into the dark and deep black
pupils, which showed no reflection of what was present, but images that
were strangely familiar. As she gazed up, she felt herself drawn into their
endlessness. Passion had begun seeing these eyes whenever she closed her
own in prayer or in pain. And, she had begun to search for Maurya in and
the images she brought, in her dreams.

Passion had grown dependent upon the beautiful African princess who
resembled her remarkably and wondered why her mother was always
dressed in that fashion. The princess had her same doe-like eyes, a sharp

nose that widened slightly, thick, full lips that seemed to spread across the room when she grinned, and her mother's air of wisdom and respected eldership. Her frame was thin, but what Passion found strange, was that she always appeared to be with-child.

The first time Passion saw her she thought she had woke up dead. Her reaction caused Maurya to grin, and Passion to calm curiously. She gazed into Passion's eyes allowing a peak into the infinite and connected with her spirit. Passion's conscience appeared to be talking aloud to her, in her own voice. It first warned her of the plan Musa and Hannibal had to kill Brother. She was told to warn them to abort it, but she was afraid to speak and kept the warning to herself. She could have saved them both had she believed what she heard or saw, but she hadn't. She was secretly thinking that she was losing her mind with grief. Passion had figured Maurya was a result of weariness and a desire to see her Mama once more. Mama Lettie had told her how people often saw their loved ones right after they had died and not to worry. But once they were caught, sent away and killed, she never doubted the spirit again. She let it guide her whenever Maurya offered and kept this part of her life a secret.

"Passion, your babies should've seen you in action today! How come they're not here—you usually keep them in the war zone."

Everyone laughed kindly or nodded in agreement.

"True–true,"

Passion quickly forced a smile on her face and hoped no one realized how far away she had been in the time that just passed. But everyone knew she had a habit of drifting and attributed it to her many loses—especially Justice having left her so early in life. They all admired Passion for her strength and they earnestly loved her. She knew that and was thankful for her people. They had helped her through the rough days too.

"I don't know y'all," Anne began almost shamefully, as she stared out of the window at the landmarks of the route her children would adjust to in the fall, "I have to say, I'm a little nervous about my children coming out here dealing with people who hate them everyday. I mean…I know it's the best thing for them, but that nasty-looking Hitler man scared me. I never told my babies about *that* kind of hatred. I never saw it that close before.

"Our Mama's and Daddies did though. They were scared through it all but they kept fighting."

Passion was preaching effortlessly.

"We've been scared for 300 hundred years,
Sister—300 years. Now they're scared too. White folks are so scared of us, they're not comfortable with us being around unless we're looking or acting like slaves. That's why we had to do this today. Whitestone won't ever forget these black faces."

Individual conversations were sparked by the brief sermon. Many began to discuss the riot, others Herzog, some the police and how brutal they had been; some were still surprised about how they narrowly escaped. But then one-by-one, each discussion paused. The bus driver had come to a full halt; the bus was standing two blocks before the el, still within the boundaries of East Village. He had put the yellow bus in park and was shaking his head in disbelief and tightly clutching his transistor radio, staring at it as if it was giving him a personal message. Reverend Mitchell had moved to the front and was standing before the driver. He spoke softly to him and placed his arm around the fifty-something year old man and lowered his ear to hear the secret. When he raised his head and straightened his contorted body, every face in the group was intensely focused on Reverend Mitchell. A feeling of anxiety and discomfort had entered and the entire bus braced itself as the leader began to unveil the mystery. He was shaken and had trouble clearing his throat. It came out anyway,

"Uh, brothers and sisters, what we experienced this morning at Whitestone, I'm afraid was just the beginning for us. The news Brother Williams has heard on the radio affects all of our homes and all of our families. It appears that a white officer has shot and killed a black youth right here in Browns' Village. Right now, right up Sutter Avenue, our people are protesting, rioting, looting..."

He continued although they all gasped, held one another, began to cry or just sat in shock. A deafening silence permeated throughout the bus; looks of fear and worry began to be drawn on each face as they all envisioned images of their loved ones and prayed to God for the safety of each of their families.

"Did they say anything about injuries or arrests?", one woman asked, afraid to suggest they should all listen.

Neither the driver nor reverend answered. So they all looked at the driver, holding the small medium they wished could be a crystal ball revealing the answers that would ease their anxious hearts. Their heads leaned forward as they were all perfectly still, hoping the small radio would tell them they need not fear. The reverend broke the spell.

"We do know that the looters are burning and looting stores on Sutter Avenue, so we will have to take Blake or Dumont. We'll park behind Powell Street for all those who live in the Sutter Avenue complex. I'm asking every brother to take each sister and child home. Walk everyone to the front door. Make sure each saint is safe and inside his or her residence before you leave.

"No problem Rev.!", shot out from the back of the bus as Brother Williams shifted gears to apprehensively continue the trip into Browns' Village. Every face was filled with concern; small, nervous chatter had begun amongst them, but Passion was too quiet and her face was ghost-like. She stared anxiously out of the bus window at each street they passed; she envisioned Sutter Avenue and her children running down the street as they did most days. She closed her eyes and pretended it was morning and they were where she had left them—in front of The Dew Drop Inn, bopping their little heads and industriously shining shoes, forgetting to even wave when she yelled, "Bye babies" from the bus. "I should have taken them with me," she reprimanded herself whispering. Connie and Anne heard her and glanced in her direction with concern. In her daydream she changed the scenario to ease her conscious. She pretended everything was fine. She saw their smiling faces as she recalled the conversation she would have had with them if she had only known.

"Come on y'all, I changed my mind, you can come with me." She imagined saying, shaking her head, disagreeing with their pleads to be on their own for the day and work. "You're coming with me—and that's that!", she wished she had said. Passion opened her eyes and allowed the tears to roll down her cheeks as she desperately fought the feeling that something terrible has happened. The boys had looked so happy when she had watched them from the bus. And her girls were just beautiful. They had looked so cute with their matching pink and white polka dot short sets with the matching ribbons. She could hear "Lester Leaps"—Papa Joe's favorite Lester Young cut from the "Bird Meets Pres" Live album, playing loudly down Sutter as it would most every morning. Something told her Sutter Avenue would never be the same again. And, she felt a strange tugging at her heart, and an odd longing to hold her children as if they were all babies again. She could hear them calling her. Then she heard Deuce. Him and his kisses—"Mommy, Mommy, Mommy, Mommy," which jolted her back into the present.

"Brother Williams!" she yelled out somewhat loud and desperately, "... please take Sutter anyway. We—we've got to see what's happened."

"Anybody else feel that way," the reverend asked. "I mean, as long as it is safe and no one is afraid..."

"Let's see reverend!", another voice agreed. Many others nodded in agreement. They were afraid of knowing, yet afraid of not knowing.

"Well we done escaped once already today…guess ain't no sense in being scared now," Bro. Williams eased under the el back into Browns' Village as if he expected the entire neighborhood to blow upon crossing its threshold. The streets were uncommonly quiet and empty. Not a soul was going in or out of the train station. Pete was nowhere in sight. His shop, usually opened until 7 was now wearing a large white sign with bold, red letters reading, "**CLOSED FOR BUSINESS**". And it seemed as if Pete had passed out signs to every storeowner on the avenue. Red, bold letters began to appear every few feet and from every store. The cleaners read, "**CLOSED FOR BUSINESS**," Freddy's Drug Store," **CLOSED FOR BUSINESS**," the Laundromat and candy store–"**CLOSED FOR BUSINESS**." It looked like the showdown scene from "High Noon," but the freedom fighters knew all Hell must have broken out.

No song cried forth from any anxious heart. No head dared to turn and look out of the quickly locked bus windows. They all had learned from the Whitestone experience, that it was best to duck under the seats right about now. Without warning those just thinking to duck were forced to the floor of the school bus to join their comrades beneath the green seats in response to the unexpected gunfire that rang out like a canon further down Sutter Avenue. Knowing they were only two short blocks from The Dew Drop Inn, Passion was ready to run. She had to see. She had to know.

"Go." the voice said to her, commanding her spirit. "Move! Go–NOW!"

"Hold–up Pat, don't go. I know you feel you gotta go, I know you feel you need to go. But don't do it Passion, you could get hurt. You won't be no good to your kids dead."

"Connie you know I'm going, right?"

"Well I'm going too!" Anne was right behind Passion on the floor. "I got your back"

"Me too. Let's just do it."

Connie, Passion and Anne jumped from the back door of the yellow school bus and ran as fast as they could towards The Dew Drop Inn. Passion, moving at top speed, was in the lead. They all had their children on their minds—especially their sons. But as they were about to approach Christopher Street, the corner before The Dew Drop Inn—Passion grabbed her stomach as if she had caught a huge cramp—and dropped to the ground. A small yet very angry crowd just a few feet away, barely noticed her as they chanted riotous language on behalf of her son.

"Come on Sis—we're almost there."
"Passion—you okay?"

Passion hadn't fainted but had felt as if she had been hit in the womb with a stick. And she knew it was Deuce. She hollered his name as she lay on the tar-covered street. As she had sat in the bus allowing herself to slip into the spiritual realm, she had felt him. Felt him like she had when she had birthed him. He was the biggest baby she had bore, and he was a breech. They both would have died if it weren't for Mama Lettie who had literally turned him right-side up and untangled her umbilical chord from around his neck. Passion could sometimes imagine the excruciating pain from recalling the memory, but today she felt it. She felt that same contraction that had reached its peak when Mama Lettie's magical hands reached in, and within a millisecond, had grabbed, jerked, twisted down and yanked out Deuce's head. Passion's eyes rolled back in her head—again. Her mouth hung open expecting breath to stop coming in or out. Then she screamed as her second son's body was pulled from inside of her. He faced her wide-eyed and screamed right back. She had known at that moment he'd spend the rest of his life being turned around, and now, someone had yanked his life right out of hers. She knew this as she arose to face the pain.

RAPE

Obscene in thought
    murderous in deed
one by one
    they're killing the seed

        Not just Justice and Deuce
    but passion, patience, love and truth
        leaving hatred, pain and disease
    empty pots and welfare cheese

Obscene in thought
    murderous in deed
one by one
    they're killing the seed

    krooked kop's the modern klan
that's why we call him "the man"
    Disguised as protectors
petty-cash paid funeral directors
    collecting high expenses
from our powers and rights, all six senses
    demonically dividing causing destruction
giving guns to junkies with lethal instructions

Obscene in thought
    murderous in deed
one by one,
    they're killing the seed

Wrists of a people cuffed to the bedpost
cocked gun to the head
but what hurt's the most
is the smack filled penis that plunges and thrusts,
poisons at first and then devours
just about everything that used to be ours.

C. Wright-Lewis 8/9/99

CHAPTER FOUR

▼

"RAPE"

BROWNS' VILLAGE
Same day
Afternoon–Evening

Within the next ten minutes for Tres, delirium and oblivion had set in, "My brother's dead", it slowly rang aloud in his head, but his mouth` could only whisper, "…my brother's dead, I'm responsible for my brother, and my brother's dead."

His mother's voice resounded loudly in his head as he recalled and relived her scolding him when Deuce had been lost during a Summer Day

Camp trip to Coney Island. He could see Passion's face, her disappointment in him–her fire, "You're the oldest!" she had screamed, "You are
responsible for your brother whenever I am not around–is that CLEAR?
You are your brother's keeper!"

His face became contorted; cringing in contagious pain as his drooped
head resigned, "and my brother's dead," he whimpered. Tres had begun
crying aloud–unashamedly moaning and mourning. He could see Deuce
standing before him; that charismatic grin and wide, always-excited look
in his eyes, his wooly afro, and his skinny arm holding on to the loved
appendage that ironically caused his death–his basketball. It was worn and
beaten, with only a faded line left encircling the brown sphere. It was
tucked underneath his arm, and you would have had to been the best on
the block to get it from him. Tres was crying, then smiling, shaking his
head almost violently at the ghost of his awkward, loveable, incredible
brother standing before him as he always had–ready to play ball.
"I want my brother," he sobbed like a baby, "I want my brother." Tres
reached out as if he could actually touch the memory. He drew back his
empty hand and wrapped his arms around himself pretending to hug
Deuce as he had earlier. He sat there rocking, trying to understand how he
could go on without his brother, the only one who really knew him. The
only one with whom he could share his fears and nightmares of Brother
the Junkie, of being killed like their father and grandparents–of losing his
mother. He reached again for his best friend and baby brother who were
now eternally untouchable.
The many bystanders cried with him–some touched him–some spoke
softly, attempting to console Tres' crippled heart. One elder sister was so
moved that she went as far as to cradle him in her arms as if he was her
own newborn baby–his spirit appeared just that broken. At last, Papa Joe
was seen carrying Tres; it was assumed that he took the grief-stricken and
shocked boy home, but Papa Joe felt it best to take him to his secret quarters–far away from the madness. He held Tres tightly and caressed the

small 13 year old, who had fainted in his grandfather's arms the second he picked him up. A tear spilled from the old man's eye after he was forced to blink. He had carried Justice in arms this way when he was thirteen too. A fly ball had hit him while he was watching a baseball game at the park and was knocked unconscious.

Papa Joe wished Deuce were only unconscious too.

"Hell of a rite of passage for a black man," he thought, "Damn!"

Papa Joe checked the time as he flicked the channels on his black and white nine-inch TV. Set. His mind kept replaying the scenario in the record shop. "God damn cops," he whispered to himself as if someone could hear. "God damn pigs!" A half snarl and a half frown held up his tears. It was now six o'clock and he was flicking from channel to channel to see if the neighborhood was still standing. He was distracted by the ruffling sheets behind him.

"You up boy?" he asked softer than he was used to speaking. Papa Joe's heart was still kind of stuck in his throat, so he sighed deeply, subconsciously shook his head in despair, and turned back to the television. He couldn't stop thinking that there must have been something that he could have done to prevent this—something he should be doing to protect his family—his family, which he had somehow failed. He had been a hero to so many and on so many other occasions, but he couldn't protect his own from their unpredictable fates. He was a war hero, had stopped a lynching in 1928 and rid the village of a butcher in '38, but the devil had still beaten him.

After sleeping for 3 hours, Tres had begun to stir.

"NOOOOO!" he forced the unconsciousness to return when he heard himself crying out, not wanting to wake up. Flashes of Deuces' dead body—his head full of hair soaked in blood—and the cop who shot him standing there, waving his gun, unsure whether to aim it at himself or at the angry crowd were ultra-vivid, inerasable images in his head.

"Put that gun down boy", Papa Joe had told the cop, "...no one here is gonna hurt you; we know it was an accident".

"Bull SHIT!" an infuriated neighbor had yelled, "Let's take him OUT! An eye for an eye!" An Afro with shades stood behind the man speaking, and showed that he agreed. The cop stood there shaking, still waving his firearm nervously. He couldn't even hear Papa Joe speaking as calmly as he possibly could, explaining to the crazed cop that he had to surrender his weapon. That he was now a murderer and had just killed his grandson. That he had started a riot and had to be instrumental in diffusing it, or all of Browns' Village would erupt. Papa Joe had spoken as rationally as he could but the cop was deafened and blinded by fear. He appeared dazed and suddenly noticed the many portraits and posters on the record shop walls. His attention was lured away by Jazz greats like Charlie Parker, Lester Young; Blues greats like Bessie Smith, Fats Domino, Fats Waller; even, Rock and Roll pioneers like Chuck Berry, Little Richard and Chubby Checker. They all began to close in on the claustrophobic cop. The elevated muses began to play for him in a slow 2/4 beat on congas, djembes, shekeres, and the other African percussion instruments strategically placed around the room; the popular dotted quarter and 3 eighth note rhythm was dancing in the confused officer's head–UUMMM BA BABA'–UUMMMBABABA'- UUMMMBABABA.'. He saw himself surrounded by African jungle bunnies, dressed in grass skirts, wearing hideous medicine-man make-up; blood dripping from their freshly cut faces for the ceremonial kill. They closed in tighter and tighter. He ultimately saw himself tied to a giant rotisserie, broiling like the huge pig that he was, with a big-ass apple stuffed in his mouth.

"C'mon man, don't look so scared. We don't eat no pork; as a matter of fact, we're vegetarians." Papa Joe was wanted to laugh and cry at the same time, he was fighting the insidious anxiety himself. But he knew how dangerous a scared pig could be, so he used his unique ingenuity and there in the middle of chaos and murder, he had folks laughing. He knew he'd have that gun in a second. He had been moving in closer and closer to him and could now place his hand gently on the officer's arm without him even feeling Papa Joe. Before a reaction could occur, Papa Joe had gripped the wrist with one hand, and snatched the gun out with the other. Everyone exhaled. Even the cop seemed relieved. Still scared and shaking, but relieved. At least he knew he wouldn't be dinner. The Afros surrounded, and then apprehended the cop just as he partner ran into the shop as if it was rehearsed thinking he was being attacked. Papa Joe had passed the gun down to the tallest Afro who continued to pass it out of sight. They had done it so swiftly that no one had noticed.

In the meantime, the murderer's partner was entering, pulling his gun from its holster, prepared to protect and serve his own. He had practically run over Tres trying to get inside.

Then he damn near started the riot all over again by yelling into his walkie-talkie,

"We need back up in here–Sutter and Stone, Sutter and Stone–Officer down! Officer needs assistance–10-13! 1 0-13!"

Papa Joe had become furious. That was all he needed–for this frightened pig to start tripping all over again.

"Everything is under control off-a-sir. *You* need to calm down."

"No! You need to let go of that officer of the law you have in your custody. That's a police officer now let him go!"

"We ain't letting go of nobody. Don't you think you need the facts off-a-sir ? Nobody hurt this pig. But he did kill my grandson. You know—the dead body you just passed over to get in here! That's who needs the ambulance, so get one here RIGHT NOW!"

Tres hadn't heard the whole conversation, but he did hear the "right now". His mind was racing. He was trying to remember what had happened, but all could hear in his mind was the loud shot. All he could see was Deuce's bloody body.

"I'm sorry about the shooting sir, but the alleged murder of the child will have to be determined in a court of law. Now where is this officer's firearm? How do I know that one of you didn't shoot the boy?"

Papa Joe hadn't even heard that last part, and could care less about what the cop was saying. He had gotten a glimpse of Tres from the window and had rushed outside to get him. Tres was covered in his brother's blood and still hugging the dead body. He was hysterical. Papa Joe knew he had to get him out of there. The brothers would handle the cops and the shop. Mama Lettie was just showing up to go in the ambulance with Deuce. She had left the children with Miss Ernestine, down the hall. As Papa Joe lifted Tres, he could see a yellow bus coming down the hill into Browns' Village. "Passion's home," he had thought. "Jesus, I don't think I can take this scene." He had known he'd catch up with her at the hospital or under the el, later on. Tres shook his head violently three or four times. Pretending to be asleep was making him restless. He decided to get up when he began to hear Papa Joe talking with someone. At first he didn't hear the other voice and figured his grandfather was on the telephone. Then he heard a deep voice, much deeper than Papa Joe's—and his was deep—but this voice sounded younger—it wasn't raspy like Papa Joe's. Deciding to lie down and just listen seemed to be a good idea since Tres didn't really feel like talking himself. Maybe he could hear something about his mother or Deuce. Maybe they would say Deuce was saved by a miracle. If he'd lie still enough—maybe—just maybe. He listened.

"I wanted to off that cop Pops. I still want him. What'choo wanna do? You know I'm your man." The voice had an eerie seriousness. It was deep and dry. It possessed deadly anger.

"I'm still deciding. Did y'all find Brother the Junkie yet? That fool's the cause of all of this. He's the reason the damn pigs were sniffing around The Dew Drop Inn in the first place. They keep him and his junkie friends in supply and demand our asses in return. He thinks he knows what we're doing and leaked some crap to the cops that ain't even true. That's what's kicking my ass. We don't even deal in drugs—everybody knows who's bringing the drugs into our community. And they know why. They know it too. Damn pigs. They know our strength is multiplying. They're just trying to take us down. You remember what that pig said when he first walked in the door?"

The Afro imitated the pig.

"I'm here for The Black Power meeting. Where's Huey?"

"Where's Huey, hmmf. What they know about what's happening out in California? Don't tell me this ain't know set up. I don't blame Brother Hakiim for going off on that pig. But they can't even say he threatened him."

"Hell no. All the brother did was recite the Constitution."

"If the pig had a search warrant that would be one thing; this was plain harassment. He had no reason for pulling out his weapon."

"That's why Hakiim pulled his."

"Let me have that piece now. I'm saving this for court. He can think he's getting away with killing my son if he wants. I got his ass. If he lives that long."

The afro handed Papa Joe the police officer's firearm and Papa Joe's face was beginning to break as the anger swelled within him, turning him red. If only Deuce hadn't returned right then for that ball. Poor baby. He never stood a chance. "BOOM!" The shot resounded in Papa Joe's head. He could see Deuce's shocked face at the sight of the gun—then his body lifting off of the ground from the closeness of the impact—then he was gone.

Papa Joe finally cried. "I never even held him—I see him so clearly. He was calling me and looking right in my eyes when he left. God."

Tres was listening as the uncontrollable tears returned. He thought about *his* last touch. Deuce had felt so warm; he had thought he was still alive for a moment. The reminiscence caused Tres to look down at his bloody dashiki. He hugged himself again, slowly took it off, and then lay back down. He tried to remember more, but all he could see was men in white trying to pull Deuce from him. He had given them a good fight–that he remembered well. He had kicked one right in the nuts. He recalled his anxiety–not knowing what to do. "I should kill that cop! Kill the pig!!" he had said to himself over and over–loudly, then shouting. He had seen a glimpse of Papa Joe. That's all he remembered. Needing more, his mind raced back to one o'clock the day before. He and Deuce were on their way to the day camp to pick their sisters up.

"Hurry up Deuce, we're already late. That mean lady's gonna tell Ma we picked the girls up late, either that or Mecca's gonna tell."

"You know it. Let's race Tres. I'll take the back staircase and still beat you to the first floor."

They had run and laughed all the way down the stairs, out the lobby door, and down Sutter Avenue hysterically. Tres smiled to himself, swallowed his tears and thought about how he bragged about winning.

"What I tell you son, stick with me and I'll make you a man."

Deuce had looked at him with the pride and adoration he always openly showed his big brother.

Tres decided to keep that particular picture of his brother in his head forever; that and the one of Deuce shooting the b-ball from outside. He would be so proud when he watched Deuce play basketball. He would do nothing but talk trash and make money. He heard himself.

"You see that shot he made? That's *my* brother! Go head–dunk it baby! It's your world." He imitated the men he heard when they played. It was something they both enjoyed doing out of Passion's earshot.

"It's your world Deuce," he repeated in a whisper.

He didn't want to be heard, but he continued to listen. He could still hear the deep, dark voice.

"Look Pops, I know nothing can bring Justice or Deuce back, but we can damn sure get some justice right about now. The people will do anything for you. After you left the shop, people just went off. There were about fifty people inside and all of them, I mean, brothers, sisters, old people, young people–they just bum-rushed the pigs. We couldn't even control them. And Brother David Walker–he came in with Passion. And they both lost it. After she went to the hospital, he held those pigs hostage for at least 2 hours. He got away too. Pigs flooded the streets and David disappeared. Man, I don't know who is protecting that brother–he can get out of some jams. I heard he was the same way in 'Nam."

"Damn, I guess my shop is finished."

"No Papa Joe. The brothers would never let that happen. All is cool."

Papa Joe looked at him surprisingly, but seriously, then they both turned to the t.v. which was then showing what used to be their beloved community. They hadn't owned much outside of the Dew Drop Inn, but it had their color, their smell, their flavor–it was their home; and now it was burning. Right outside, Browns' Village was burning and they couldn't stop it. From Papa Joe's home on Powell Street, behind the projects, they watched the madness on television. Reporters darted in and out of flames and fights and asked asinine questions to looters and asinine looters gave interviews on "The Six O'clock Action News". The chaos made them feel like it could have easily been the last day in time. False liberation was visible and it permeated throughout the city. People in Bedford-Stuyvesant, Crown Heights, even folks up in Harlem were rioting. They had all had enough and just had to let it out, let it off, get it off. Everyone Black–no longer colored–appeared as runaway slaves who raised up to burn the life out of modern day slavery; *and, get a few goodies while the gettin' was good.* People who had never stolen in their lives took advantage of the unwatched, open door; slipped in with a friend, and ran out with carpets gripped to their shoulders, 19 inch televisions on their backs, stereos, bikes,–even living room furniture. Fire caught the hearts of frightened and fed-up people, and caused some to even steal a life in cold blood because they knew no one would see–either that–or they just didn't give a damn anymore. This was revenge–revenge for Deuce, for Justice, for Emmett Till, for Medgar Evers, for Nat Turner, for David Walker. Hell, for everybody! The village was temporarily insane. People were inundated with the monster's hatred to the point that they had become the monster themselves.

"Any snake will do!" they shouted. Once bitten, any snake will do!"

The concrete in Browns' Village bled, and the sky burned. It left the stench of fearlessness, contention, fear and pain. Screams of laughter and retribution were mixed with screams of grief and dismay. Other-wise life-giving, radiant variations of yellow, red, brown and black skin was possessed by blinding riot lights which gave birth to a different energy–one of unquenchable rage.

Most residents were home though, afraid to experience the modern day uprising. Not everyone wished to witness the numerous arrests and beatings that were being made of those you would least expect to see chained up. They watched their neighbors, friends and relatives on t.v. and prayed for the morning to come soon. Papa Joe knew it was time to make his move. Loving and overly concerned neighbors could sometimes get you killed for your sake. But before he could awaken his remaining grandson, Tres and many other Browns' Village residents were jolted out of their sleep by a thunderous explosion that shook every piece of concrete in the neighborhood. Many grabbed their children out of their dreams, ran down staircases and fled into streets, fearful of potentially collapsing buildings. They had always heard that New York could never geographically be considered earthquake territory, but those who watched the shaking earth beneath the rising flames that briskly moved through every other store on Sutter Avenue easily disbelieved that truism. The cleaners–gone. The luncheonette–gone. Freddy's Drug Store–gone. Nothing would ever be the same again. Even The Dew Drop Inn was partially damaged. Two brothers stood in front of the shop all night to guard it from looters and fire bugs. Someone had heard old Joseph Justice say, "We'd rather see it burn," and thought they would oblige.

Two deaths had been reported and twenty-five severely injured persons were taken to Kings County Hospital. Unity Hospital, that small hospital on St. Johns Place, had run out of room for the 75 other victims of chaos and chance—fear and opportunity, victims of out-right criminals, and victims of other victims.

Three syncopated explosions went off and caused every Dan Rather and Walter Cronkite wanna-be to emerge on the scene. Each was alliterating foolishly into hand-held TV cameras while helicopter lights chased some of Browns' Village's best sprinters senselessly. Brother the Junkie's sorry ass was in the street too. He was on the corner of Belmont and Rockaway Avenues, directing traffic as if nothing had happened. No one could understand why drunk or drugged men felt it necessary to fulfill their civic duty by standing in mid-traffic on the busiest of thoroughfares. Nonetheless, there he was—stoned out of his mind and pointing the way. Brother knew good and well everybody would be seeking him out after Deuce was killed. And, being a junkie, he did what any junkie would do. He got high and pretended nothing was wrong. He didn't know how he always ended up getting someone from Passion's family killed. He really liked her. He had loved Justice too. But he couldn't think about that now. The *white lady* always made things *all right*. They would hide out together for a little while—and then everything would be fine.

Papa Joe and the Afro could believe their eye when they saw Brother the Junkie on the news. Not only was he on channel 2, but he was interviewed on channel 7 as well. Ironically, one sensationalist after another asked him the same thing—"How did this all start?" Papa Joe knew Brother the Junkie wasn't stupid enough to tell them the truth. He packed a bag for the night.

It was funny how Brother the Junkie was caught on different stations, but had not been seen by the Afro who wanted him most. No one saw the tall Afro either, as he slipped in and out of shadows looking for the

notorious junkie. If he had found Brother the Junkie this night, that
would be one dead brother. The Marines trained the tall Afro wearing
shades in the dark, 20 different ways to kill with his bare hands and he
had developed a special combination just for Brother the Junkie. Now
atop a 14 story roof, over-looking all of Browns' Village he could see
everyone and everything. The last of the looters were still scattering, the
pigs and firemen were consoling all the white people. Mr. Bernstein was
a wreck; his wife was hysterical. Pete the Barber was pitching a bitch
about his broken barber's pole; he told anyone and everyone who would
listen of its significance and symbolism. Many never knew that barbers
had been considered physicians in history, or that the big red and white
candy-cane looking light had meant so much to Pete. The value of
Browns' Village's culture illuminated in the fire, then it singed and
appeared to fizzle out. It was passed midnight and people were still walking around, shocked and dazed. The bird's eye view spotlighted Anne,
searching for Passion. The Afro turned in a military pivot and sighted a
shadow on another roof top, a few buildings to the east. He was on one
of 12–14 floor apartment buildings. Anyone could hide there. Turning
further east and looking downward revealed the familiar half bop and
half stagger belonging to Brother the Junkie. The afro dripped with
sweat, and his heart beat almost stopped.

Below, everyone, still recovering from the explosions, had admired his
beautiful work,

"It looked like the fourth of July."

"The sky was the prettiest gold and red colors—it was breath-taking."

"*Child*–I thought it was the rapture; it looked like the end of the
world."

"Burn, baby, burn," the tall Afro commanded slowly before he faded out of sight.

"BOO–BOOM! BOO–BOOM!" before that next BOOM came Papa Joe had been standing in front of the boy who was playing possum. He was visibly nervous and was shaking Tres as hard as he could.

"Come on little brother, we gotta go".

"I wanna wait for my Mama, Papa Joe."

"Don't worry, she'll know where to find us, she's been under the el before."

"I feel like we're all dying Papa. I'm afraid. Can't we go find my Mama now?"

Tres was crying again. So Joe just held him as hard as he could. And as he did, he whispered to him softly, yet confidently, to have no fear. He told Tres that in spite of all he had been through, his ancestors had it much worse. He additionally explained that he was bone of their bone, and flesh of their flesh. That in order to survive, he had to trust him and trust God that he would see his Mama and his family before daylight.

"Everything is gonna be *all*-right."

The "*all*-right" had come out so smoothly; it had calmed Papa Joe as well. It was as if it wasn't even him talking. His voice was so healing. It reminded him of someone else. He couldn't place the voice, but he had known it well. And, everything *would* be all right. He knew it in his heart. The afro and Tres were both looking at him as if he was crazy, as a foolish grin took over his face. It was brought about by impromptu memories of Justice—and his old friend Reverend Franklin—Passion's dad. He could suddenly smell them and feel their presence.

In a sheepish, apprehensive voice Tres asked, "Are you okay Papa Joe? You look funny."

A screaming siren startled them all as it flew passed. They hit the floor simultaneously at what sounded like another bomb going off next. It was so loud,, it sounded as if it was coming through the door.

"Time to go," Papa Joe was shoving Tres through the door. "Next thing you know, they'll be coming for interviews. Either that or they'll be blowing my house up too."

The Afro disappeared before Tres could think to say good-bye. He had his mission, and could envision his success.

"Where are we going again?" Tres was trying hard to keep up.

"Under the el."

"What's under the el train?"

"It's not what, but who. Miss Hannah's place is under the el and I'm sure the only thing burning under there is some food. She sure can cook."

Tres followed closely in the old man's footsteps, through alleyways he never knew existed. And he thought he and Deuce had covered all over Browns' Village. They never looked back, nor did they look up at the fiery red sky. At times gunfire and sirens seemed to surround them, inciting flashbacks of wartime in Papa Joe's head. He sweated as he had 40 years before, dodging in and out of fox holes and traps set by the Japanese enemies, strategically he had danced over land mines disguised as old tires in the abandoned lot they passed through. He had saved hundreds of women and children during his tour, but received only one medal, nightmares and bad memories in return.

Unable to see himself inside of Papa Joe's shadow, Tres felt safer and calmer than he had all day; he saw Papa Joe differently from before too—taller—stronger—more like his Dad—Justice. He noticed as they walked at the quickening clip, that his profile fit within the bearded shadows almost perfectly. And, that their movements were exactly the same. They both walked like N.B.A. players, whose shoulders moved like a lion's when pacing masterfully through the bush, circling up, then around like a carousel pole. They even breathed in the same pace.

These revelations gave new meaning to the name "grandfather" for Tres. In awe, he watched and mimicked Joseph Justice Freeman, and knew who he would be just like one day. He watched his grandfather and realized why he was a respected, but dangerous man; why his father and brother were both murdered, and why he must stay alive—they were of rare and royal stock. And, their mark was bound to influence the world.

"I expected y'all hours ago," Miss Hannah stated flatly as Papa Joe walked through the door. "You know I heard everything. It's a damn shame. Go on in the back wit your boy, we got some food waitin' on y'all"

"Hi Miss Hannah", Tres felt safe saying.

"Hi baby", she sang, "…lookin' just like your Mama".

Papa Joe never spoke. Didn't have to. Miss Lucy, Hannah's right hand for the last ten years, was in the huge bright white and stainless steel kitchen, frying fish. Hannah had been her savior when Lucy had lost everything she had. She had been around for most of the last twenty. Big-Hip Hannah's had become her sanctuary and her home.

Year's back, when the projects had first been built, the new city-owned high-rise buildings had given the neighborhood a new urban look. They had over-shadowed and encased the small town ambiance country-like shops and homes had once given Browns' Village. Once erected, to everyone's surprise, they had even surpassed the el train which provided a convenient means of transportation, getting anyone to the city within half an hour. Yet, it caused new darkening shadows to be cast over the growing community of sun people.

Big-Hip Hannah's Bar was built two blocks south of Pete's Barber Shop, under the el. It was right next door to her ever-popular Rib shack, but was notorious for the no-account, raucous-causing heathens who attended, partied hearty, drank, and then fought throughout the night—especially on the weekends. No decent churchgoer would be caught dead within a half a block's radius of Big-Hip Hannah's. They fried their fish and chicken and barbequed their ribs at church and looked down on anyone they heard had been under the el. Nonetheless, if some one just happened to have been craving some of Hannah's ribs, or her infamous, mouth-watering macaroni and cheese, and after purchasing it, just had happened to kind of fall into the bar where a shot or two of whiskey ended up poured down his throat, it wasn't seen as a desecration to the community. Not of course, unless that he, happened to be a she.

It was an unwritten understanding that a man could lie drunk in the street, get up, dust off his clothes, and still be called Mr. Brown. But let it be a woman found lying drunk in the street; she'd be disgraced for life. This was Poor Miss Lucy's story. She had always been known to be a nice, clean, hard-working woman. Unfortunately, she was smitten by Country Tim, a truck driver from her hometown Durham, North Carolina. He had come to Browns' Village to visit her for the first time. He was all decked out in his Sunday best, right off the truck. He came talking big-time, cat-daddy talk, flashing all kinds of green, and asking everyone to "slip me some skin", gliding his hand in and out of conversations. Miss Lucy had been real proud to be seen with the newest cool cat in town. And she had become the envy of all the women. She had started to hang out at Big-Hip Hannah's like she was a regular; drinking, smoking, and dancing dirty until dawn. Country Tim had a lot of fun with Lucy. They had truly fallen in love, but at the end of his two-week vacation, he had to get back on the road. And, unfortunately for Lucy, she had begun some habits she couldn't afford, but she couldn't seem to shake either. She would be seen staggering out of Big Hannah's almost every night. She would just be reaching home through the shades of dawn, when most early shifters were leaving out for work. Most folk hadn't noticed Miss Lucy's destiny heading towards Skid Row until the grapevine made it known that Lucy had gotten her pink slip. Then the worst came. Fat Back, Hannah' s brother and partner, was seen picking Miss Lucy up off of the sidewalk. Most folk, including Big Hannah, began to completely shun Lucy, who had lost her "Miss," and become "Old or Poor Lucy." She could barely get a "Good Morning" out of most. Women just shook their heads or rolled their eyes when they'd see her coming, while the men looked the other way during the day, many of them were seen slipping up to old Lucy's apartment late at night, and slipping out in the early dawn. She had needed the money, so she gave them her time. Poor, old Miss Lucy had become a legend in her own time. Women began to caution their daughters' daily, "to keep from under that el 'cause you're bound to wind up like poor, old Lucy." The grapevine later reported that Lucy had even lost Country Tim. He had stopped through Browns' Village two months later, and heard of Lucy's ruined reputation. When he returned in another four months, he wasn't able to recognize his once sweet Lucy. Word was that everyone had had her, but nobody wanted her. He hung around Big Hannah's for the weekend, hoping to get a glimpse of Lucy, and when he did, he couldn't believe his eyes. Through with big-city life, he jumped in his rig without even checking out of the bed-n-breakfast he loved so well, and headed for the interstate.

Big-Hip Hannah, on the other hand, had somehow received a mythical reputation as a hard hitting drinking woman though she had never actually been seen drinking or drunk. Folks must have just figured that since she sold booze, she drank it too. She had always been loud. And was witty enough to slice you with her tongue in a heartbeat. Her size was part of the reason too. Big-Hip Hannah was all of 300 pounds and about 6 foot 2. But she was just a big, black and beautiful businesswoman from Buford, South Carolina. She wanted a piece of The Big Apple and wasn't leaving town without it. She also knew the power in owning property and started shopping around in Browns' Village as soon as she arrived. After meeting Papa Joe one day at the luncheonette on Sutter Avenue, she decided to take his advice on buying cheap property under the el train. Once that el had been built, the dollar value had dropped immensely. No one wanted to live under train tracks, but there was no better spot for a bar or a speakeasy. Hannah was known for saying, "Folks don't hear the trains walking, when the music is talking." Big-Hip Hannah's had also been built far enough away from the residential part of Browns' Village that Hannah could get away with a little raucous and criminal activity without the neighbors calling. Her reputation had also been rumored as gun toting and gun selling, and even a little drug dealing. Most didn't want to believe that part; after all, there was no proof of it. They believed it about Fat Back though. He was a lot bigger, and a lot meaner than Big-Hip Hannah. He was the bouncer, her partner, her brother and confidant. Little did most people realize, Fat Back didn't do anything his big sister hadn't approved. No one in Browns' Village messed with Fat Back. His reputation for tossing people out of Big-Hip Hannah's Bar with no sympathy was notorious. Even his eating habits had been known as bad; he had gotten his name from sucking down more gristle and fat with his ribs than anyone else could stomach. But there was one thing all the party people loved about Fat Back; he always kept things exciting at Big Hannah's; he out-drank folk, out- danced folk, out- sang folk—Fat Back did it all.

Whenever someone had heard the phrase, "under the el," it was automatically understood that something was happening at Big Hannah's. In the early days, it had been entertaining to hear and tell stories about one's adventures under the el. Papa Joe had quite a few. Even Passion had told her children about how she was once literally hit by a man who the infamous Fat Back had thrown in the street. He had spoken to her as they were all entering their building one-day and the children asked how she knew him. Fat Back was a giant to the children, and Big-Hip Hannah was a myth. But here Tres sat, in Big-Hip Hannah's, expecting to see the giant at any moment. He wondered how they were connected to Papa Joe; and, how they fit into his plan. He knew Papa Joe had a plan.

Tres also found himself in a flashback with Miss Lucy. He knew she looked familiar, but he didn't quite remember why. She saw him looking at her and smiled. She piled a whole mess of collard greens on his plate, right next to some fried catfish and potato salad. Tres wasn't really hungry, but knew he should eat. Papa Joe went back in the front of the bar to speak with Hannah, leaving the two to get to know one another.

"Thanks for the food Miss Lucy."

"You welcome," she said a bit nervously, not quite knowing what to say to the young man who had been through so much pain today. She searched her mind anxiously, trying to think of something encouraging, but all of her stories seemed too bitter and old for his soul. Then before she could sweep through her memory banks any more he began speaking.

"Were you there today Miss Lucy? I mean. Um. I think I remember seeing you today when it happened."

"Damn," she thought. She really didn't want to recall the murder herself. She was probably crying and sleeping as much as he had, trying to get it out of her head. She stopped breathing for a second, and then resigned, "Yes honey. I was right there with you. And I'm so *so* sorry," she said as if it was her fault.

"Yeah, I'm a miss my brother. He was my best friend in the whole world. Do you have any brothers or sisters Miss Lucy?'

"As a matter of fact I do. And you know. . " She was recalling unexpectedly, and her mouth was speaking without her permission, "...my oldest sister once told me the legend of Maurya and it changed my life".

"Who is Maurya?"

"Well, she was a slave, and she lived about 200 years ago. To tell the truth, she kind of reminds me of your mama. I mean her spirit, the way she was strong and just dealt with what life gave her."

Tres was listening intently, especially once Lucy mentioned his Mama. Lucy could see that she had his attention and since her spirit seemed to be flowing, connecting with this young brother, she told the tale as it had been told to her.

"The lightless sky was so dark against the water, one could not separate sky from sea. Maurya could envision her dark body gracefully slipping into the dark, still waters. "No one would see me," she thought feverishly as her eyes rapidly scanned the ship's bottom; "all is black."

Within the passed two weeks she had lost her loving husband, her family, her friends, her homeland and—her dignity. God hadn't been answering lately either, so it appeared that Maurya was now godless too. All that was left was this infernal kicking in her belly she was determined would not live in this world.

Within the last 48 hours, Maurya had watched her captors rape, torture and murder her fellow captives, the women on either side of her perish, and herself engage in desperate acts of escapism she would never have even imagined. Just ten minutes ago, once she had been certain that death had freed her cuffed sisters, she had chewed dead bones and flesh from their hands and feet, monstrously gnawing and spewing until she could loosen them from her chains. Nauseated by herself, she realized she had become the animal her captors were training her to be. Unconcerned with the transformation, she convinced herself that, amongst all the other lost elements that comprise her being, her spirit had been lost as well.

Maurya had lain as stiff as a stiff herself. She covered her work as the last drunken, white demon stumbled over her during a final futile attempt to fondle. "I must wait," she whispered to herself, and did so until all was deadly still.

After falling more times than she could count, sometimes hard and flat upon the corpse of a slave or a silent beaten radical, she miraculously managed to find the stairwell leading from the stench of life in slavery, to the salty air freshness and freedom of death. She abruptly threw herself against the stairwell wall at the distinct sound of light footsteps behind her. Had she misjudged the demon? With fear she reluctantly turned her head to find five fellow prisoners following her, apparently with the same plan in mind—suicide. She continued through the maze-like ship, all the way to the deck and embraced the darkness. But then, finally faced with the moment she had been praying for, Maurya was blinded by the darkness and confusion.

Her furiously beating heart caused her chest to heave as she listened to the sharks below discuss how to divide her into portions. Unconsciously rubbing her slightly protruding stomach, and staring into the hypnotizing, black waters, she began to reminisce of the day her village had the Great Celebration of Life, announcing to all that she, the princess-queen, was about to bring a life forth. The very same life she was now about to end. The wife of a young wealthy chief, and a descendent of the Great Queen of Sheba, Maurya and her seed were destined for great things.

The last of her line, she had been the only one who could possibly carry the royal seed. This life had been a blessing from the one God over all. Her village and all surrounding villages had come together, dressed in their finest garb, bore gifts of untold treasures, and offered ambrosia. She could still hear the music, rising cadences of joy and rhythmic drums with powers to possess. "Oh, and behold the dancers!" she murmured in her native tongue subconsciously. She could feel them glide by, floating like happy gazelles, extending their acrobatic bodies to one another in mid-air. All were happy, and all was bright. And, the one was stood most radiant was Maurya's father—the king. He knew that the prince he had chosen eighteen years ago, was the perfect choice for his princess—someone from intelligent, warrior stock—one who would fulfill the prophesies and produce a descendent as wise as Solomon, who would indeed one day, "Bring the past to the future, bring wealth and freedom back to Africa", as the oracle had stated to him.

"Bring the past to the future, bring wealth and freedom back to Africa..." Maurya heard herself whispering, and then repeated it louder. Arousing herself and staring into the water, she sees the old prophet and hears his voice," Your seed will bring Africa back to Africa."

She frantically looks about with disbelief.

Her followers no longer awaited her lead and had begun diving into freedom. Still gripping the railing, with one leg already over it, Maurya realizes that she cannot jump. She could see the prophet staring into her eyes; feel him squeezing her hand helping her back over the side, echoing the heart-rending words. And as her spirit is rekindled, atrocities beyond belief had been taking place all around her.

With desperate hearts of their own and the inspiration of the most desperate, once God-fearing people, were now literally yanking, tearing and gnawing limbs to break free. The sounds of bodies splashing into the ocean incited the man-eaters and wailing, grief-stricken bound slaves awakened the drunken demons.

The captain, the only sober demon aboard, flew from his quarters armed with his pistol. He lighted the sky, and yelled at his chattel as he fired in the air, forgetting that they wanted to die. Breath-takingly, he became awe-struck by the beautiful African queen backing slowly away from the railing. He interrupted the overseer's whip from painfully guiding her back downstairs, and in the distraction lost three more captives to the sharks.

He beckoned her to him with the same entrancing voice that sobered his subordinates and commanded them to salvage his livestock. But, she could not move.

"Bring her to me!" his demand had caused all to freeze. She didn't know what he was saying, but she knew what he wanted. And, despite her protruding belly, he took her. He christened her Dinah, and kept her as his own. But he refused to keep her babies.

Maurya made a conscious decision to spread her seed. She would go on to birth six children; five of his and the very first. Captain Gourmand would keep her captive upon his ship for the next eight years. And every child she bore was sold on different land. But she knew, in her heart, that this same seed would come forth from these new and strange lands, unite, save their people and return home one day."

Tres had eaten every bite of the delicious, cornmeal-coated whiting that tasted just like his Mama's fish. He realized how relaxed he had become as he sat looking into the former beauty queen's eyes with fascination and understanding she hadn't expected. She smiled and wisely nodded, fixed on his stare in return.

"So I'm Maurya's seed?" he smiled when he asked the question, though he already knew the answer.

"You know it baby,…you are Maurya's seed. Now the question is…what are you going to do?"

The question provoked a revelation within Tres. He had never thought of his life's mission before. His most adult-like position had been to always help his mother, brother and sisters, insure their well being and safety. Now that Deuce had died Tres was pretty sure that the job was more than he could handle alone and perhaps there was more that he should be considering. His eyebrows frowned and caused his eyes to squint as he stared into the new friend across the table. What was he going to do?

Sirens continued to blare interrupted by the less frequent explosions. Every store owned by a white person had been severely damaged, victimized by the tall afro's rage. Miss Lucy and Tres exchanged worried looks as a fire engine noisily clanged passed them en route to save another building from burning to a crisp.

"RAGE"

Bloodless hearts filled with fire
Destruction is their one desire
One blind cop kills one black boy
Now the entire village we will destroy.

Hate in their eyes, heat in their hearts
They'll find the culprit severed in parts
But will his life truly compensate?
We've lost our future in Deuce's fatal fate.

Paralyzing pain from wasted pregnancy
Erupts in emotional despondency
Then evolves to evoke an awakening
From death comes life comes death you see.

Bloodless hearts filled with rage
angrily turn the history page
and close their eyes to committed sin
the village now buried—devastation welcomed in.

C. Wright-Lewis 7/26/99

CHAPTER FIVE

▼

"RAGE"

BROWNS' VILLAGE
That Night

The hospital scene had been too much for Mama Lettie. The madness, the panic, the anger and the pain had reduced her to tears–unstoppable tears a bawling child would usually shed. She had decided to wait for Passion in the lobby; she was bound to be dragged through the swinging doors any minute now Lettie thought, but she never was.

"The shot heard 'round the world, the shot heard 'round the world, the shot heard 'round the world", sang in Passion's head. That's how a witness had described it to her. Passion couldn't forget the tone of the woman's voice, nor the look of painful astonishment she wore as she expressed her sorrow for the loss of Passion's baby boy.

"I'm so sorry, honey," she had said as she shook. "We all saw the officer who did it. Murphy's his name. We got him locked up in the record shop. It sounded like the shot heard 'round the world. I knew it was bad. I ran out of the cleaners, and there he was. Standing there with the gun still in his hands. Poor Miss Lucy saw it all. She's just a mess. She'll testify though, that's for sure—she'll testify." Passion had listened, but couldn't respond at the time. Now she couldn't get the woman's words out of her head. *"The shot heard 'round the world.* Connie and Anne had held her up. Then they held her back as they brought him out. She looked at that cop and lost all of her senses. They took her to the hospital, and asked that Passion receive a sedative to calm her, then they called Mama Lettie. Connie went home to take care of the children while Mama Lettie headed to the hospital. Anne took care of the police business while Passion was supposed to be resting. The drug fought with her anguish and lost.

Passion would close her eyes and see herself sitting there on the hospital stretcher, like a black dot sitting in the middle of all that white—her clothes unkempt, shredded in some places, stained with Deuce's blood from when she had held him for the last time in the ambulance; she had actually held him all the way to the hospital. Everyone knew he was dead, but she insisted on taking him to the hospital. She had raised Hell because they took the white cop to the hospital first, leaving her baby boy lying in the street. But they told her that they wanted to avoid having two dead bodies. That had been the last straw all together. Her eyes became permanently angry, slanted and red; her face was all dirty with sweat, her broken shoe heels making her limp, her afro was just mucked up. "All I need is a straight jacket," she admitted to herself. She knew she was out of control. But she couldn't change a thing. She felt completely power-less, until she remembered that the officer was in the hospital too. And she planned his demise. The nurses and doctors had left Passion alone after giving her a dose of Valium. She sat and waited for hours, red, black and blue with grief she thought she would never dine, dance, or sleep with again.

"I thought we had a deal," she told God, "I thought I filled my quota. Well, I'm very sorry Lord, but someone's got to pay."

Mama Lettie had just arrived, she sensed Passion strongly, and she kept getting visions of Passion in a crazed state, destroying everything around her. She was whispering lowly, hoping Passion could sense her as well, "Come on Passion, and walk through those doors. Come on Passion, come on girl. But David Walker came out instead. He sat next to Mama Lettie, then reached out and hugged her as if she was his own mother.

David had run out of Whitestone, jumped on the train and actually beat the others back to Browns' Village. He planned to go straight to The Dew Drop Inn to report to Papa Joe. He saw himself descending the steps and heading towards the record shop as he sat in the corner of the train, half asleep and half conscious. Then his keen senses made him sit up straight as Malik, once known as Chris; and Fred, both his good buddies from 'Nam approached him. They spotted him the second they boarded the train at Broadway Junction, transferring from the Manhattan "A" train. They were laughing at the thought of sneaking up on him which they knew was an impossibility and he was laughing too. He knew what they were thinking.

"Chris–", he laughed aloud as he spoke, "...as tall as you are brother, I can see you with my eyes closed and blind-folded." He stood up and greeted each with a strong hug.

"We sure didn't expect to run into you brother. What happened to the protest?"

"Man, the pigs almost had my black behind going to jail–me and a whole lot of other brothers and sisters. If it weren't for Passion Freeman, I would be on my way to Riker's Pen for sure. That sister is too much. We gotta strengthen security on her. I don't want nothing happening to Justice's widow y'all; she's definitely our strength."

Chris bent into a 45-degree angle in order to sit on the pale yellow, hard, straw-like seat. He wanted to hear better even though the remainder of ride was only 2 stops. He was becoming completely consumed by the story–especially with this character Herzog, David described–he may be someone they would need to nullify, he was thinking as they stood to get off of the train.

"...So if they still give us a hard time about sending our children to that school we're going to have to be out there in full force–*strong* man, like a *real* army."

David was angry all over again, and the brothers couldn't agree more.

The three Afros walked in rhythm down the hill into Browns' Village. David, Malik and Fred were shaking hands on the matter and discussing how to present it to Papa Joe when they stepped into The Dew Drop Inn. Malik thought about what David had said about protecting Passion as he watched Deuce run into his hip. The energy that touched him that moment would stay with him forever.

Malik's face flashed across David's mind as he sat there holding the elderly woman like a child. He remembered how distraught Malik had become in Viet Nam when his company had been sent to destroy a village still occupied with families. A little boy–9 or 10 years old ran right into him, just like Deuce had, but he was holding a baby in his hands. Out of sheer confusion he had just run to the right kind of soldier. The boy was trying to save his baby brother as his mother had instructed before he left her to die. It was none of his business, but Malik had felt it was his obligation to take that little boy to safety and blew up a couple of mine fields to do it. David knew Malik was having flashbacks. Fred was probably with him. Fred was still enraged too. He had his legs paralyzed during that same tour, but he was fortunate enough to be walking today. His physical paralysis had been temporary, but the mental paralysis appeared to be eternal. The bloody nightmares and flashbacks frequented him several times a day and he was in the early stages of heroin addiction. David suspected, but hadn't approached him about it yet. He looked down at Mama Lettie and wiped a tear from her face. "And where the Hell is Passion?" he asked himself, searching his mind for the right scenario.

"Let me walk you home Mama Lettie–*please*. I promise–I'll find Passion and bring her home."

She didn't want to go, but she knew she couldn't stay. More than anything other feeling, Mama Lettie felt she had failed Passion somehow. Guilt-filled thoughts haunted her, insisting she should've kept the boys in sight, or at home or that she should have demanded that Passion stay home–*something*! Her dreams had shown her the blood and the cop and the boy, but she had not the nerve to believe it. She just wanted to see Passion's face, hold her in her arms like she did when she was a little girl. She knew Passion was wounded beyond repair and how much she was needed by the only person she ever called daughter; she just *had* to touch her and let her know they could live through this one too. She couldn't forget hearing Passion's painful cries the day they buried Justice. Mama Lettie thought they'd end up burying Passion too. At first she had tried to be strong for her children's sake, but Passion just lost it once she saw Justice lying there in that black coffin, dressed in his white African holyday garb, his drum set atop his missing hand.

"I can't believe we're going through this again," Mama Lettie spoke into David's eyes, "I just can't believe it." One of the doctors who took Deuce's body in came through the swinging doors. "Is anyone here from the Freeman family?"

"Yes," Mama Lettie quickly answered.

"We can't seem to locate the young man's mother. She must have left the hospital, she's no where to be found."

"Is Deuce—the little boy, really dead?"

"Yes ma'am, I'm afraid so. Are you his grandmother?"

"No. Not really, but I've always taken care of him".

"We understand ma'am, but we really do need next of kin. Is it possible for you to locate the mother and bring her back to the hospital? We need her to sign some papers. She could come back in the morning if necessary, but please find her."

"Are you sure she's left the hospital?" David asked baffled by her disappearance.

"We're very sure sir, maybe she left before you came in."

They looked at one another, with question marks across their faces. Mama Lettie held David's hand; and the two left slowly and reluctantly.

Minutes later, Passion appeared before the officer as he lay in the sectioned off part of the hospital. In an instant, she attacked him with all of her pain; her surprising blows to his closed eyes kept them closed for months, impaired for years. He would lose his blood for the blood she had lost. For her parents—for her brothers—for Justice. And when Deuce's face entered her head she screamed so loud, she almost didn't hear the people running towards her voice. He knew she was going to get away and grabbed her with his free arm. Passion elbowed his eye, extending its injuries. Sweating bullets with her heart banging in her chest, she ran as quickly and quietly as she could and slipped out of a side door. Within seconds cops surrounded the building on Sutter Avenue. They were actually inside of Passion's door when Mama Lettie arrived and thanked God the kids were with Connie. Mama Lettie had made David promise to come back for her as he slipped away from the cops; she was sure she knew where to find Passion. In the meantime she told the press what they didn't want to hear and asked the nation—"How long are we going to allow white people to get away with killing our children?" They swiftly moved the cameras to someone else when she began to remind everyone about Emmet Till and other young, colored male victims throughout the years who died during Klan picnic- lynching throughout the North and South.

David was listening from a distance. He smiled proudly at the words of truth and power from the elder until he spotted a hiding addict in the corner of the building, revealed when a huge spot light was turned on by the National Guard. It illuminated the entire area, making midnight into midday. Un-pulled window shades were quickly drawn, leaving just enough room to see what was going on below. David slipped on a newspaper as he changed his temporary post and turned his thoughts to Brother the Junkie. He remembered Brother as a boy. They had been in the same class in school from the third grade, all the way to the seventh grade. Brother's last name was Wilson, so he usually sat right behind David. Observing someone from one seat behind for four years can teach you a lot about that person. He knew Brother and Brother knew David too. They had shared many friendly and unfriendly moments together, the majority had been secrets they didn't even discuss between themselves. They had an unspoken respect and familiarity simply because of their last names. David had been the only one to hear the nasty remarks their many teachers made throughout the years regarding Brother's shabby clothes and his sometimes-foul odor. They would often embarrass him when whispering questions like, "Can't your parents afford to buy you anything new? Or "Is there running water in your flat?" Until Brother got his gig as a paperboy and was able to contribute to the family wages, he often appeared unkempt and disheveled. Most of the children would dog him about it when his older brothers weren't around too. He really didn't even tell his brothers when someone teased him. He knew that after they would come to his rescue, they would beat him up for needing their help. The other kids had started so many rumors about Brother's notorious brothers; they scared themselves away from the lonely boy. David remembered how much the lonely boy had changed once they left Junior High School 266. For a while he was known as the shoeshine and Doo -Wop king. A natural tenor, he often harmonized with the best of them. But then he changed. He ran away from home and was working at Big Hip Hannah's. He still kept the paper route for a while; up until everyone realized he was robbing them all blind 'cause he had gotten strung out on that smack. Everyone blamed Big Hip Hannah. How could she let that happen to that boy, they wondered. But it wasn't her fault. She didn't even know what was going on until it was too late to help. Fat Back was the one who had turned Brother on, then turned him out.

Brother had always heard that under the el was the place to see a lot of hip cats in fine clothes and fine women wearing tight dresses. Like other teenage boys in the neighborhood, he lied about going to Big Hip Hannah's and hanging with the grown folks—laughing and smoking and drinking! They all would lie, and they all knew it. But Brother decided he would make his lie the truth. So he began sneaking out of the first floor window, as he had seen his older brothers do a hundred times. He left the overcrowded bed he shared with his four younger brothers, the over-crowded room, which included his four sisters and embraced the night air. Once he did it, he knew he would never stop. He felt so free. No one he knew was outside at that time of night. No one he knew was hanging out at Big Hip Hannah's.

He never went inside, well at least not until the day Fat Back made him a man. Brother would just hang outside of the side window. He sang along with the band or the jukebox. He rooted for the under dog during the fights he thought were better than anything he had ever seen on television. He wished, when watching the fast women with big behinds and revealing cleavages, that he could someday hold a woman like that in his own arms. He'd stand there dreaming of fast women and fast cars and fancy clothes until a patron would spot him. Then he'd get thrown into the street every time Fat Back was able to sneak up on him. It had become a ritual between the two. Fat Back really like the young boy he knew was too young to be out so late. He often wondered why the boy's folks never came looking for him. After the first six months, he stopped chasing Brother so much and would slip him some ribs, or allow him to hang for a set when a famous band was playing. He just couldn't let him come in because Hannah would lose her liquor license behind minors being in the place, and she would never forgive Fat Back for making her lose her business.

The day Brother turned sixteen; he went to visit Fat Back in the middle of the day. He had decided that he was old enough to drop out of school and lead his own life. He stood before Fat Back and spoke in his deepest voice,

"Fat Back, I want a job. I ain't no kid no more. I don't want to live my life delivering newspapers. I want to work for you."

"Oh, so you a man now?"

Brother stood firmly. But inside, his heart was skipping beats.

"I know what you do. I mean besides being a bouncer. I see you make connections and I figured, uh, I figured I could help."

Fat Back didn't respond at first. So the two just stood in the middle of the street, under the el, for what seemed like an eternity to Brother. Then Fat Back slapped Brother as hard as he could and watched him fall to the ground.

"So what is it that I do?"

"You don't do nothing but bounce. I didn't see nothing man. I swear, I didn't see a thing."

Brother had begun to cry. He tried to get around Fat Back so he could run down Van Sindren Alley, but the 6 foot, 7 inch, 400-pound man gripped him like a bear.

"As long as you don't see a thing, and you don't know a thing, you can work for me. But if you make one mistake, I won't know what happened to you."

Brother was nodding his head as hard as he could to indicate that he thoroughly understood, because he sure couldn't talk. He was still crying too. He was half happy because he had gotten what he wanted, but his was more afraid than he had ever been in his life. He had no idea of what he had gotten himself into. But he reassured Fat Back as often as he could say,

"I'm your man Fat Back. I got your back."

David remembered the fancy clothes Brother started to wear when he first started working for Fat Back. Brother was stupid enough to think it was still a secret after he bragged about it to a few guys he used to sing with on the corner. He didn't have time for them now. He had a job. Then his parents threw him out when they learned he had dropped out of school and had been under the el mostly every night. That's why folks thought they were helping poor Brother out, still buying the Sunday paper from him while he was casing their homes, setting up robberies.

David's instincts were accurate as usual. He spotted Brother slipping into the back door of the building across the courtyard. He knew Brother would be there for a while. Junkies don't shoot up and run. David frowned in Brother's direction; underneath it all, he really felt sorry for Brother. He knew he was just another victim. He laughed at the irony of it all as he thought of the nickname people refused to stop calling the perpetrating victim despite how notorious he had become—"Brother." To tell the truth no one had a special reason for calling him "Brother." Everyone had called him Brother because his family had.

When Paul was just a baby himself, he showed so much love and concern for each baby that came after him, and so much pride in being a big brother, his parents taught the babies to just call him Brother. Soon the whole family called him Brother. But David remembered that teachers always called him Paul and Brother seemed to like that a lot. As the number of babies steadily increased, resulting in 13 children all together, 9 under Paul, his personal time with his parents decreased, and Brother began to resent being "Big Brother." He felt invisible. So when he escaped he really never wanted to return. He wanted to be Paul, not Brother. But people never stopped calling him Brother; and he never stopped calling himself Brother. He hated them for it, but he mostly hated himself. David realized this as he watched the madness erupt outside of Passion's building. He was waiting for signs. One that would tell him how to find her, and one to tell him what to do about Brother Paul.

As dusk crept into the picture of panic and mayhem, neighbors warned those who just coming in from work to, "Hurry up inside, cops been shooting folks!" The temperature had lowered, but the intensity of the anger made Browns' Village's vibe radiate as if it was still 98 degrees. The Afro recently home from 'Nam was still at work. Every 20 minutes or so, a thunderous explosion would shake the community as if it contained a mine. In the meantime, Brother was reminiscing about the first time he met his beautiful lady. He waved his hand in the air, as he re-enacted how he stroked her gently as she had sung to him that very first time. He had shared his very soul with her, admitting that secretly he liked being called Paul, though no one called him that anymore. She vowed to always call him Paul and she would be his Paula. Then they sang, *"Hey, hey Paul—I want to marry you...hey, hey Paula, I want to marry you too...- my, my, love..."*

His heart raced. The small, aluminum foil shook in his hands. It had been one year, two months, and twelve days since his last fix, and each day he had gone through the agony of hearing the lady call out to him,

"Paul—come back". He had stashed it there, inside the broken pipe, under the staircase, after a pick-up six months ago when the pigs broke into Big Hip Hannah's, beat the daylights out of Fat Back and took him to jail. He had to close his eyes and still his heart to stop the shaking. He feared Fat Back even from behind bars. He could still see Fat Back's eyes staring at him, his cuffed hand wriggling his wrist so he could point his index finger toward his throat to signal death to Brother. Fat Back never spoke when the pigs dragged him through the door; he just kept giving Brother the death stare.

"Don't worry Brother," he remembered the pigs saying, giving him away completely, "this guys going to jail for a long time. He'll never get to you."

That was all Fat Back had needed to hear. He squinted angrily at Brother as Brother dropped his head. "I'm your man, Fat Back, I'm your man!" Fat Back yelled, "Remember that—*Brother?*"

Fat Back's voice had drowned the song out. *"Bro-ther"* began to resound in his ears louder and louder. *Bro-ther! BRO-THER! BRO-THER!!* The explosions outside were only fizzles in the distance. The haunting of painful memories were all that existed in Brother's world. His third grade teacher—Mrs. Saperstein—had always referred to him as the dirty boy to her colleagues. He heard her one day while he stood outside of the teacher' cafeteria, too nervous to go in and ask her to call his Mom because he had wet his pants. It had hurt him to his heart. Teachers aren't supposed to call you names, he had thought. *"Dirty Boy!* Now he smells too!" She had made them all laugh.

"Dirty boy!!" "DIRTY BOY!!!"

Well she was nothing like the white lady he loved. She loved him despite his flaws. She never called him Brother, or Dirty Boy, and she made him feel so, so good. Brother's hands were vibrating so violently he couldn't open the packet.

"Sshh!" he angrily commanded the bad memories to leave his head.

"Come on Paul…it's been such a long, long, time", she sang like a seductive goddess, *"Hey, hey Paul, I wanna marry you, hey, hey Paul I want spend my life with you.*

"Be still," he whispered, *"please,* be still." He breathed deeply; tears forced their way out of the closed lids and slid down his face. He breathed deeper still, again, then again. Twice more, he forced the air to move slower from his expanded lungs, up and through his nostrils, and then finally he could open it.

He tested the white powder with the tip of his tongue. It quickly deadened every sensation in his mouth. The welcomed death then thinly spread over his face and crawled up into his head. Simultaneously, it raced through his veins, down his throat and into his heart. His skinny knees buckled, landing him in the trash-filled corner of the exit way. He was ready.

"Hey, hey Paul, I want to marry you…"

After momentary unconsciousness, an air of scientific seriousness came over him. Brother's eyes whitened and widened. His breathing regulated, becoming steep and steady. His mouth tightened into a frown and refused its usual twitch, then, determined to remain focused; he channeled all energy to the hot spoon, the needle and the syringe.

"My—my love…my, my love…"

His grin grew as he slid the needle out of his re-opened, favorite vein, then clumsily he dropped it at his side. His mind and body slid too, farther and farther into down and into oblivion. He looked dead, lying there like a stiff in the morgue, drool sliding down the corners of his mouth; but in his mind, Paul and Paula were singing and he was walking down the isle, dressed in white, with a white lady on his arm. Her beautiful, blonde hair blew in the breeze as she glided through the white daffodils that covered the grassy floor of a beautifully decorated backyard. An orchestra was

playing, and his white teachers were all there, applauding, crying, congratulating the happy couple, and calling him Paul.

A small boy who dared to take the back staircase against his mother's
orders viewed his life-less body from the flight above. He ran to tell her
about the dead man in the basement stairwell. Fellow junkies often
shunned by Brother once he had cleaned up, sought revenge when they
heard. They knew he wasn't dead and they knew there was nothing he
could do to stop them either. They ran quickly down the steps. They
laughed with glee as they took his shoes, his pants and his shirt. They took
his filled wallet and fought over the cash it held. They took the corner of
heroin left in the foil packet Brother had used to escape. They even took
the new needle and syringe while Brother laid there watching his dream
turn into a nightmare.

The sweat began to pour off of his head as the white lady disappeared;
she turned into dust she really was, right before his eyes. The music died and
the temperature rose. Fat Back stood before him like God Almighty with the
judgment book in his hand. He held it high for Brother to see. The words:
"MURDERER" and **"THIEF"** were written in capital letters and in blood.
They were at the top of a long list of offenses which wore his face and called
their names out to him–*"Deceiver!"*–*"Pusher!"*–*"Liar!"*–*"Back stab-
ber!"*–*"Blackmailer!"*–*"Adulterer!"*–*"Forger!"*

"You did it too!" he yelled back at Fat Back , "you taught me how!", he
cried.

The words melted off of the page and became Fat Back clones. They
marched towards him with blood dripping down their faces. They carried
machetes that threatened to behead him. He ran into the street in his
sweat-drenched underwear, fleeing from himself. The brightness of the
riot lights knocked him to his knees. He covered his eyes and crawled to a
nearby garbage can and dug out some ragged trousers and half torn shoes.
He headed to Rockaway Avenue where he used to doo-wop on the corner.
Half stumbling, half falling down Sutter Avenue, he sang his part in a

crooked, hoarse voice "Silhouette, sil–o wet–sil–o–wet- Ahhh–oohh…"
He was ready for his debut.

David was right on the case. He had been watching the backdoor for
Brother for the last two hours from Mama Lettie's apartment. He was
hoping that Passion would slip through the pigs and media hounds, and
make it upstairs. He knew they hadn't found her because one pig was still
stationed in front of the building. He would patrol the area every half
hour, moving through the lobby to the back of the building and back to
the front. And, he and Mama Lettie could hear his loud radio sending
instructions form his commanding officer. David had given some commands as well. He advised Connie to hold on to the children in her apartment, and had Anne handling the police and the media. She was down at
the precinct filling out reports on the officer who shot Deuce and giving
the media all of the horrific details. Anne was to meet him at Big Hip
Hannah's after she left the precinct. He was certain the Papa Joe had Tres
over there, and hopefully, Passion would be there too.

At first Anne was surprised,

"Big Hip Hannah's Place? You sure Papa Joe would be over there?"

"Where you been Anne, everybody's been up there but you. Hannah
and Papa Joe are old friends. I believe he's the one who helped her get the
restaurant in the first place."

"I think you got your facts confused, the Papa Joe I know wouldn't have
a thing to do with no boozing and drug-pushing."

"Well of course not. Big Hannah ain't into that mess either. That's all Fat
Back's doing. You need to get *your* facts straight. Look, just meet me there.
Once you meet her, you'll know the deal. Ain't that right Mama Lettie?"

Mama Lettie gave Anne the nod. Anne shrugged her shoulders.

"Whatever I need to do, I'm mo do. I'll be there."

It had been an hour since then. David and Mama Lettie had discussed what needed to be done, then waited for him to make his move. Once the pig stepped back in front of the building, David was out of the back door, out of the light, and into the darkness. And, Mama Lettie was still in the healing business, she was on prayer detail.

As soon as they were both gone, she opened her secret bedroom closet and changed into a beautiful, white gown. She tied her head in an African cloth made of a shiny white and gold mixed taffeta, then adorned her neck with her white spiritual beads. She lit incense made of frank and myrrh, anointed her- self with a special oil, and began to chant and pray. Mama Lettie believed in more than just the Christ spirit; her grandmother had taught her that her ancestors could and did protect and guide her everyday of her life. Only they could reach Passion when she could not, though she would never stopped trying. Almost before she shut her eyes, she envisioned Passion in a frenzied state, running down a dark street. So she imagined a circle of white light around her, guiding her home. "Be safe child, and come home," she repeated again and again. Lettie spoke to Passion, as if she was sitting right there in the large closet next to her. She reminded Passion to spiritually arm herself, then literally put her arms around the young woman she loved like a daughter, and held her as tightly as she could. Lettie felt herself giving Passion all the energy she had within her own body, all the determination she could muster, and all the power she could generate. She didn't stop until she felt the sweat dripping down her back.

Then she envisioned Mattie, Justice and Deuce; she could see each of their faces clearly. Mattie's long, dark face and large eyes were as peaceful as ever, Justice's chiseled, handsome light-brown skin and slanted, Nelson Mandela-type eyes almost closed due to his big grin, and Deuce's young face was grinning just like his Dad's, as usual. All their eyes seemed to be speaking to her, telling her that all was well. In her meditation, Lettie then began to travel to the past, to happier days and times. She began to see the young Reverend Franklin and the young Joseph Justice. They were sitting around her kitchen table eating fried fish as they always did on Fridays.

Everybody was eating except Mattie who was pregnant and ready to give birth to Passion at any moment. She was experiencing mild contractions and refused to eat the fish Lettie seasoned just for her so she wouldn't need an enema before delivery. Lettie was the mid-wife and never left Mattie's side. She was just as excited about Mattie's baby as Mattie was, especially since her little boy had died. They were all excited about the new baby, but tired of waiting.

Lettie decided to take out the homemade wine she and Mattie had stored since before the men came home from the war. She smiled to herself as she watched them once again, sitting around the table laughing, eating, drinking and telling stories. The story she needed to remember then began to be voiced loudly through the two men who swore the women to secrecy. It was what had cursed both their families for the last 40 years.

"Hold my hand Mattie," the reverend insisted," I need you to understand what I'm about say." She stared at him strangely as he squeezed her hand with one of his hands and rubbed her big belly with the other. "My real name is Justice Joseph Freeman and that man over there, is the real Joseph Franklin."

Mattie frowned and pulled her hand out of his.

"*WHAT?* ", she and Lettie screamed in stereo.

"Stop playing Rev., you always pulling somebody's leg," Lettie squinted at him and shook her head as she filled his glass with more wine. Mattie was just staring at him, speechless and confused. She didn't doubt he was telling the truth; she was just baffled as to why. She was shocked, but couldn't move. It was like the baby reacted for her. It visibly moved and kicked in her belly, and caught everyone's attention.

"Look at the baby", the young Papa Joe said, as he picked up Justice Junior and allowed his small hand to touch the unborn foot moving horizontally across the blue and white dress. "She must know it's true."

"Are you serious," Lettie asked as she sat.

"Let me explain," the reverend began. "*Well,*" the young reverend always used a long southern "*well*" before he started a story- during the story–actually, all through the story, " y'all know that we met in boot camp, then were sent over to Europe together to fight in the war. Well, fighting crackers had always been like fighting Nazis–you know that. We just wanted the chance to show that we were the men to take 'em down. But, those white boys were so jealous of any success we had against the enemies, they made life pure hell for us. "Well, there was one captain in particular. His name was Gourmand. I had known of him from back home in Mississippi. He came from a line of brutal slave masters and Klansmen. Everybody knew Gourmand. And they also knew how he kept slaves way after the Civil War–probably has some right now. Their slaves never had the chance to run–they stayed chained every moment of their lives. Matter of fact–they were in the chain-making business. The only slave to ever leave was a woman named Maurya–she was considered a legend and was one of the first slaves brought on the plantation. Cree Indians helped her escape back in 1810. The Gourmand master then had been her personal captor and ship's captain. They say he kept her on the ship for years, sired and sold all of her babies on every stop of the Middle Passage before he settled near Gulfport, Mississippi.

"Anyways, his grandson was the Gourmand I and everybody in Mississippi knew to be the one white man to castrate and lynch more colored boys than any man in the south. You see, he still had his family's plantation. And he created a product he sold to every white man who wanted the strength and power of a Negro. He called it buck balls. And that's exactly what it was made out of.

"It's a real big thing down in Missip," the name got shorter each time he recalled his home. As painful as his past had been, Lettie still recalled the way the reverend's eyes lit up when he spoke about beautiful Mississippi, " yeah, sad thing is, most colored men, 'round age 16, 17 or 18, right when their bodies' hormones gettin' their strongest is when Gourmand and his boys start their pick–a–nigger parties. Everybody comes too- relatives from out-of-town come like it's a Christmas celebration or something. They choose us and hunt us down like wild game. Then they lynch us right there in the middle of the picnic. White folks be eating, drinking and cheering while a black man is swinging from a tree, his private parts slit from his torso, his skin pulled off like a rabbit's to be drained for special oil and the stench of bloody death spreads quickly over them like a fog. It's a sick scene y'all."

Mattie, Lettie and young Papa Joe were all crying, not loudly, just quietly and sadly. Lettie still could hear the young reverend's voice continuing the story like it was the first time she heard it. She remembered not being ready for the next statement he would make.

"The reason I know so well is…'cause I was hanged and expected to be a contributor of buck balls too. My brothers cut me down. This ain't a birthmark you know." He pointed to the rope scar his neck adorned like a black, two-inch thick necklace.

"I never believed it was when you said it baby, but I never imagined you'd been strung up", Mattie spoke softly as she gently moved her index finger down and around her husband's neck. They all stared at it for a more than a moment, wondering how it must have felt to be a death's door and escape.

"I became Gourmand's greatest enemy that day. I made him look bad in front of his people. I was the first in a hundred years to escape that devil's greedy grip. He vowed he'd never stop chasing me until he caught and hanged me for good. That's why I ran here to New York. I could swear

I heard him yelling my whole trip here. His voice was so angry it was shaking when he bellowed from his big gut, "Git that NIGGERRR! Git 'EMMM!!!"

"You see, I had been atop a horse they were fitting to slap so he could run and I'd be strung. But, my big brother Sam had gotten himself a rifle, one that could hit a target fifty feet away if you were a good shot, and my brother was. He sat in the bushes for hours, waiting for my lynching time. I didn't even know he was there. I thought I was dead for sure. I had prayed and prayed and called on everyone on the other side I could remember, starting with Jesus, to send me some help. *Well*, they slapped the horse and Sam shot the rope. *Y'all*, I rode that horse straight out of town. Sam was dead on my heels, right behind me. And, Gourmand and his boys were right behind Sam for the most part, but we lost them in the woods. Them white boys were no good at riding in the woods at night. The sad part is they would catch up to him later. That's 'cause he didn't listen to me. Sam was fearless and lived like he was untouchable. I told him not to go back to Gourmand, Mississippi, but he put me on the bus with my auntie's little suitcase, packed with food I couldn't eat for hours, said he would meet me in New York in a few days and I never saw him again."

They all sat in shock at the story they had just heard—even the reverend couldn't believe he had lived through that horrifying experience.

"Wait a minute Rev.," young Papa Joe snapped everyone out of the hypnosis, "you didn't tell them about why we switched identities. Get to the part about when you meet me in the army," he had said with a proud smile on his face.

Lettie smiled too in retrospect. She envisioned him picking up little Justice Junior who was only 20 months or so at the time and spent most of his time going from lap to lap, or playing under the card table and knocking the cards off of the table whenever he got a chance. The adorable toddler was already attached to his future wife. He'd wrap his arms around

Mattie's big belly and lay his head on its side. She'd let him lay there too; she'd rub her belly with one hand, and rub his little back with the other.

"Right you are, right you are", Rev. shook off the bad memory of his near hanging death, rubbed his scarred neck, sipped a little more wine, took a bite of his catfish and continued. "Where'd I meet you boy?" he smiled real big and slapped his friend on the back.

The two cracked up laughing, and skipped to the next part of the story without sharing the little secret with the ladies. They had met right there in Brooklyn, in a little bar. It was in the same location as Big Hip Hannah's, but long before the el train was constructed. Back in the turn of the century, former slaves had moved there and lived in a row of shotgun houses the called Blackman's Flats. The former slaves turned the quarter acre of unmanageable farmland into a small community where they even worked part of the land and sold their harvest and goods at Belmont Avenue's market where they bartered with the Jews on the weekends. In the farthest corner of the land, where sleeping folks couldn't hear music late at night, was where the men had built it, just a little place where they could have a little sip after working hard. This was a good ten years before Mattie and Lettie had moved to New York. It was when both young men were free and feeling their oats, but also seriously beginning to plan their lives.

This night, they both were sporting fancy ladies on their arms, but had ignored them practically from the moment the four introduced one another. They had all attempted to sit at the same cozy booth in the back, then decided to sit at the bar. They ended up talking all night long.. Before long, the two discovered that they had a lot in common; they both belonged to the new Brooklyn chapter of the new organization that would someday be the best thing to ever happen to coloreds, according to them both–The National Association for the Advancement of Colored People, they both had the same plan–to enlist into the armed services. They shared the dream many colored men had of fighting the Germans and maybe even teaming up with the all-colored flyers they had both heard of–"The Tuskegee Airmen." To legally kill some white boys in retaliation for all was done to them was all the retribution they needed. They had felt as if they were long-lost brothers. "Kindred spirits, yeah that's what we are" they remembered deciding after much conversation and few drinks. They even had the same name–Joseph, and the same last initial. One was Justice Joseph Freeman, the other Joseph Franklin. They often joked about the women they lost that night. The women would never see them again, but Justice and Joseph became inseparable friends.

"*Well,* we both did enlist, but we didn't get to fly. As fate would have it", the reverend's preaching tone had returned," we ended up in 69th division of the Marine Corps, run by a captain by the name of Gourmand. I thought I'd be strung up all over again. This is why we switched identities. Brother Joseph here was about to be shipped out and he designed a plan to save my life by sending me in his place."

"The only thing was," Papa Joe interrupted, "was greedy Gourmand got his hands on me instead. Man, was he mad when he found out I wasn't one of the Freemans he hated so much. I thought he was gonna kill me anyway. I acted like I didn't know a thing about the reverend here, and it was just a case of mistaken identitiy."

"How could he be so sure, you two do kind of favor one another Free," Lettie questioned with a look of disbelief still on her face from hearing the amazing tale.

"Uh–uh Lettie, ain't no mistaking a Freeman. We definitely all look alike. Just like them damn Gourmand's look alike. I can smell one of 'em a mile away, and I guess they can smell us too."

"Umf, umf, umf," Mama Lettie was repeating over and over, recalling how she felt while revisiting the scene. She sat back in her white gown. "Gourmand sure sounds familiar," she thought to herself, trying to remember where she had last heard the name, which had so much blood and pain, attached to it. "Gourmand!" her eyes popped open, "Vote for

Senator Steve Gourmand, the one man for the job", she recalled the slogan that was on every billboard in town just last year during the last election. 'Hmmf, ain't no such thing as a coincidence", she said aloud to herself, reminding herself of her grandmother.

She quickly moved towards the window to spy on the officer keeping watch below. She had to get to Hannah's to see Joseph Justice. She left her lights on, but pulled the Venetian shades down, allowing the light in the living room and kitchen to seep through. She turned her bedroom lights off to give the impression that she had retired, and snuck down the back staircase, through the boiler room and out of the back door of the adjacent building as David had instructed.

"RESURRECTION"

Spiritual insurrection
will be the death
of imperfection

The village—a morgue
ghosts door to door
after countless attacks
just can't stand anymore
Nerves raw,
body's sore
like rows of shattered glass cracking
then fading,
systemically perpetuating
division from the whole
tormenting the soul
death has overcome,
what was is no more.

Spiritual insurrection
kills the imperfection
and fear of the worst kind of dejection
divinely prepares the needed injection
of lethal love
the resurrection comes from above.

C. Wright-Lewis 8/6/99

CHAPTER SIX

▼

"RESURRECTION"

BROWNS' VILLAGE
That Night

The darkness had deepened and Passion seeped sadly into the dark light. The farther she ran into the darkness of the night, the more comfortable she felt and the freer her spirit became. She couldn't hear the bomb-like blasts which exploded around her in her honor via the afro's fury; nor could she see the strange shadows of light in the sky, given off by the near, yet distant riot lights which also failed to seek her out. She was consumed by the darkness. She drank it–she ate it. She danced in it, and then she bathed in it. It enveloped her and she enveloped it in return. She needed it. She needed its vastness to cover up her pain, to hide her under its huge mothering arms, lift her up into its nothingness and lull her to sleep upon its suspension. She was traveling, speeding motionlessly it seemed. It was not her physical self-commanding her movements, she knew full well. Yet, she could do nothing to stop, or slow down. Spiraling at times, then often going straight, Passion tried to estimate the time that was passing out of her control. She knew people must be looking for her and at times wondered what they were thinking; Mecca and Zaire's faces were before her,

"Where you going Mommy, where you going?" they asked with sweet concern. She reached out to touch the colorful rope-like ribbon she had used to adorn the top of their long braids.

"I got your back", Anne chimed in.

"Me too, girl—*hermanas* baby! We are sisters forever."

Connie was smiling with courage Passion had never seen her wear. She wanted to reach out and hug her to let Connie know how proud she was of her too. Then she tried to grin back at Anne, who was seriously smiling, nodding her head in short, inspiring approvals as one would who wanted to beckon or positively urge another on, but the flight then revisited, continuous in its mission, it swooped her up, and set Passion into motion by the unexpected gust of spiritual wind, causing her mind to soar to new places.

Despite the dancing riot lights transforming Sutter Avenue into Saigon, blaring sirens filling the air aided by hovering helicopters, flashing red lights, fear-filled screaming by grief and horror-stricken victims, their vengeful friends and neighbors, and the crackling of fires burning Browns' Village down as if it were Mississippi, their flames leaping from roof to roof, lighting the sky with red and orange cautionary smoke signals, Passion passively pressed into the portrait of blackness before her. Two would-be track stars, turned looters, armed with a giant carpet clumsily stumbled and fell trying to avoid hitting Passion whom they were convinced had to have seen them coming, but never moved out of their way. They quickly and quietly repositioned themselves and the massive shag upon recognizing her. They certainly didn't want to alarm Browns' Village's well-loved and now notoriously sought-after she-ro.

Their puzzled faces awaited some form of acknowledgment from her, and then turned to fear-filled frowns when witnessing the air of strangeness and distance about her.

"Peace Sister," one attempted. "Isn't that Passion?" he whispered, " Man, I heard she almost killed that pig that shot her son. He'll never forget her...word on the street is he's blind.

"Shut-up June Bug, can't you see she's going through a bad time. Don't disturb her. I hope she's on her way out of town. Every pig in the city's gonna be looking for that sister." They were fumbling with the carpet at this point, unable to leave, yet unable to stay.

"Maybe we should help her. She doesn't look like she knows where she's going."

"Naw man, she'll be all right. I'm sure she's protected. We need to get this big ass rug out of here before the pigs come for us."

The other nodded in reluctant agreement as they re-repositioned it on their shoulders, then stood watching Passion float further into the apartment complex. Their quick gait became a fast trot as they watched her walk towards the back door of the 14-story building near Blake Avenue.

Passion neither saw nor heard them, though she had flinched when she heard the word *peace*. Her spirit read them as allies and continued carrying Passion to her destined appointment. Spirit was in control, yet physical anger was still strong enough to escape and manifest before her. Herzog had the nerve to be in her face, holding his bullhorn, spewing venom. She felt her body hit the ground as she impulsively re-enacted the scene from earlier that day. She kicked at his face, and then ducked the returning blow to her now blackened eye. As she rolled over in the grass and sat up on her knees, the thought of praying entered her head, but quickly left when she looked down and was repulsed by the blood of her other enemy, which still covered her hands and soaked her forearms.

"Pig blood," she sneered.

Magically, the moonlight grasped her attention. It seemed to be calling her. She looked up into it like a curious puppy, her head turned innocently to the side. The silvery light lured her toward the backdoor of the building that compelled her soul to enter. The door was as red as her bloody clothing and skin. She stopped to observe this coincidence. For a moment she thought rationally and wondered why this was the only backdoor in the projects painted the color red. The moon shone on the handle, so she entered and ascended as high as she could reach. The brilliant moonlight shone solely on the roof of the building; everywhere else was black. The sky was dark, yet cloudy. The clouds gave it a grayish, tin-like tint while they blocked out any other opening for it to shine through except the spot Passion wallowed in mourning.

She found herself on the roof, sitting in the circle the moon made for her. There, she went inside of herself, subconsciously like the moon, blocking out the rest of the world. Tears streamed down her bloated and blackened face, burning her skin and wounded eyes. She raised her head and opened her eyes as much as she could to face the majesty of the moon, "What now?" she growled as loud as she could, "What NOW?"

And then, feeling as if she was finally face-to-face with the one responsible for all of her problems, for all of her woes, for all of her losses, she reached back to her grandmother's birth, and the pain it entailed, to her great-great-great grandmother's cut belly when Master had ripped her unborn baby from her womb to threaten all slaves who dared to consider escape, to the cries of all of her captured ancestors as their chained bodies boarded the shark encircled ships, and, using every bit of energy she could ever had, and ever will have, she shrieked a heart piercing, tear-jerking, unnerving scream. Actually creating an image of crossed fists chained by their wrists, the sound traveled like a flash of lightning, breaking time's record as it whipped around the universe and pierced each cosmic plane. It re-opened mended wounds and once broken hearts. It awakened the ancient pain of Khem and the new pain of Johannesburg. It lasted seven minutes of 1963 and seventy thousand years of the earth's past. It disrupted the Afro's last explosion, and awakened each of Browns' Village's light sleepers.

Then, with complete resignation she yielded,

"Please, just take me. I don't want to hurt anymore. I can't lose anymore of my love. I can't lose anymore of myself."

She spoke as if she knew God was sitting beside her, pleading, feeling her requests were reasonable and legitimate, she continued, " Why can't you just stop? What more do I need to lose? Just take me now. TAKE ME NOW!" Passion was looking at the nearby ledge of the 14-story roof. She knew she was compelled to this place for a reason. She must be destined to jump.

"Almighty Creator, please. Don't take any more of me. My heart is shredded in to pieces right now. I've been reduced to a hate-filled animal. I can't do your work anymore. I cannot function this way."

Her voice was very low and sad. Her energy was gone and she couldn't feel her heart beat any longer. Her head hung down. She knew this was the end. Her body was lifeless; she could no longer smell nor see, nor feel, nor taste, nor hear. Time had stopped.

Passion waited. She expected to be driven to the edge of the roof at any moment. She waited some more. She finally realized, as she knelt in the moonlight, that she was paralyzed. She was unable to muster the will to bend her pinky. She was unable to even think of mustering the will to do anything.

"I am finished," was all she could think.

As quickly as it had left out, descending upon her in a spiraling, blue and white light, the shriek Passion had launched into the universe returned to her in a healing hum. Entering the top of her head, then permeating downward throughout her body, the blue and white light rejuvenated every cell of every organ within Passion. The mantra then awakened her senses. It filled her lungs as she uncontrollably began to chant softly and humbly, not understanding the very sound which came from her own mouth, "Ooooohhhhhhhhhhhmmmmm, ooooohhhhhhhhhhhmmmmmmmmmmm…" the universal phon of unification traveled through around her head; then through it. Following the circle of light, it engulfed her spirit and spoke to her heart, letting Passion know that she was not, and would never be alone, that she was one of many, fighting an eternal battle which she was about to be completely armored to win.

Passion sat in the Divine spotlight like a praying mantis, her arms spread wide open, her body resting on her scarred and tired knees, her head bowed, humbled, yet tingled with new life, feeling the eyes of every spiritual authority in existence. Next, a cool heat that began to warm every fiber of her being let her know that The Almighty was in her presence. She was used to spiritual experiences, but nothing touched this.

"Is it You?" she asked almost prayerfully, almost fearfully. "If you *are* here God, please tell me how I'm supposed to handle this. How do I go on from here, and why should I? I don't want to feel better. I don't want to go on. I'm so, so tired."

The clouds parted slowly and allowed the moon to descend. It lowered itself and hovered over the 14-story apartment building. Then it embraced the now truly frightened widowed orphan and mother. The blue-white light was now about her. She could see its energy illuminating about her body, although her eyes were closed. Its coolness massaged her skin and she was compelled to un-tighten her lips. A smirk emerged from the corner of her mouth and grew into a grin, then a smile, a giggle, and finally—a laugh. Then came the slightest breeze she could ever imagine. It graced the hairs of her skin ever so gently and dabbed the tip of her nose with a whiff of Johnson's Baby Powder. Deuce's face appeared before her. His presence immediately erased the horrifying, bloody image that had been imbedded in her memory at the hospital where she had last seen him. His once matted afro, soaked with blood laying atop the permanently frightened and death-filled face, now appeared to her as a picture of love in perfection. Deuce's eyes were twinkling like stars and his teeth were beaming like lights as they spoke to her,

"Hi Mama, Mama, Mama, Mama", he sang gaily, though his teeth kept bumping into his lips from trying to speak while grinning.

He couldn't physically touch her, so he made head gestures planting kisses in the air, North, South, East and West, as he had done every morning of his previous life. Her face filled with joyous tears, her cheeks puffed out and she swallowed her heart as it repeatedly rose to her throat.

"I'm okay Mama. I'm with Daddy—Grandma and Grandpa too—see!"

Her tears flowed like a flooded river. And before she could think of being afraid to look up, she could smell him again, and this time, it was really Justice.

"Oh my God..." she was trying to grasp the spirit standing and smiling painfully out of the same desire to touch, "I thought I'd never see you again."

His voice was the same, deep and soothing. It pierced her heart causing her temporary anxiety to melt. He just stood there staring at her forever with his soulful eyes. She could see and feel the white strands of energy he sent her through his force field until he was certain she had received sufficient telepathic wisdom and light,

"I'm always with you baby. I'll never leave you alone. You gotta be strong though. You must continue the fight. We're only separated for a season, pretty Passion, ...only a season."

As he spoke the palm of his right hand was circling her face, sending her the energy to heal it, drying her tears before they had a chance to fall. She closed her eyes, allowing his light to recharge her being.

"I love you so much I still feel you Justice. Your scent stays with me..."

"That's because I'm here baby, I'm always here. But I also know you're lonely. You need someone like David. You can trust him."

"David's cool..." she stopped herself realizing what he was telling her. Passion also realized his spirit had left her space. But she felt different energy. And she smelled lavender.

"Mama!" she was almost screeching as she felt around the being of light, looking for a way to get inside to her mother.

"Lord knows we raised that boy right. And you two were always meant to be, so don't worry because you will always be."

"Mama I want to touch you." Her tears had returned and were rolling through her quivering lips, and down her throat.

"Come on Passion, this is supposed to be a happy reunion."

"It is Mama, it really is. I'm just so happy you all came to see me."

"Well if we didn't, you were coming to see us, and we couldn't let that happen. Mecca and Zaire need you there honey; and we need you to be down here too." Her hands rotated around Passion's face as she spoke, just as Justice's had. Each rotation was a circle of blue light, which widened up over her face, covered her head, and then traveled down her body. One by one, Passion's bruises, cuts and wounds disappeared. Her anxiety lessened with each stroke of love, and her zealous, confident and secure spirit returned.

"Now you know I was coming to see about my baby."

"I know you were Daddy," Passion was ready for the ritual of energy transfer this time.

She even raised her hands up to receive his energy through her palms and send him some of her own. She wanted him to know she was now all right. "I know you got a pulpit up there reverend; you keeping them saints in line?"

He cracked up laughing. He held his side, bent over and let out a hollow, better than Santa Claus laugh. His hearty, old, glee-filled roar filled her heart with all the joy of her childhood. She began to laugh her self. At first Passion just chuckled at his gaiety, then she burst into an uncontrollable guffaw. When she looked up again, she could see her brothers who had transcended. Each called her name as they flew over her, laughing and sprinkling a silvery dust over her head. They were spinning and spinning above her faster and then faster. Before she knew it, Passion was spinning also. She spun in a whirlwind motion, unable to stop her movement or her laughter.

Passion's eyes were fixed on the changing moon. And, the next thing she knew, she was on the ground. Her head was still spinning and she was trying to grab hold of it. She stood up and began walking slowly. Stumbling and eventually tripping over a lead chain rope, hanging and swinging with others like it, divided by short poles for the purpose of protecting the grass around the housing development, she managed throw her hands palm down in the grass before she could land on her face. She stood up; her head was still swirling. Resigning, she then squatted and allowed her head to hang for a moment. She took advantage of the opportunity and this time was fully able to thank her God.

"Almighty Divine Creator I do thank you for salvation and my renewed life tonight. Thank-you," she was whispering now, "thank-you." She opened her eyes and could finally see clearly.

"*Where* did everybody go?" she asked aloud, not believing she could ever be alone again. "And, *how* did I get down here?" she asked herself with a little less volume, stepping away from the chain that had tripped her.

Passion looked up at the sky. She smiled and waved as she chuckled to herself. She looked at the distance she could have jumped and momentarily pictured herself splattered on the concrete. That was not a sight she would've wanted her daughters and son to witness, her friends and family, ancestors nor God to witness. She shouted another thank-you at the top of her lungs. She was crying and feeling very blessed as she continued to look upwards. Sighing deeply as she stepped away from the unforgettable scene, she couldn't help but turn and look up once more. This time her eyes caught the green and white street sign as she approached the corner. She wanted to remember her whereabouts later when she'd have to recall all of this, "What Street is this? Man, these projects make every corner look the same." Passion conversed with herself looking at the construction site across the street for even more "affordable housing." "I don't think I can afford to live in these affordable projects anymore. Most of us probably losing more than we ever have before trying to live "affordable." She spoke unashamedly to herself knowing others could hear. She still felt a bit lost, but that didn't last long. The street sign above her head read "Livonia Avenue" which caused Passion to smile. She could smell Justice too, which made her know he was still guiding her path. Moreover, her lesson for the night was not over yet.

"I guess I'm going home," Passion said to herself as she headed towards the block she and Justice grew up on—Powell Street, between Atkins and Livonia, right beyond the affordable housing and the el train. "*There I go, there I go, there...I go...—pretty baby you're the soul who snaps my control...*" began ringing in her head the moment Passion stepped on her old block.

Moody's Mood for Love was always playing loudly on the street during
her childhood. Passion went right back to the 40's. She felt her heart swell
as the familiarity of the delightful aromas that could have only come from
her mother's kitchen embraced her. The sweet smell of Mattie's double-
chocolate triple layered "black-out" cake made Passion think she could go
in her old house and actually find her Mama there in her old-fashioned
kitchen, wall paper lined walls, red roses splashed about the table cloth,
the curtains and wall paper and one red rose in a clear vase set upon the
table, stooping over the open oven door, removing some home-made bis-
cuits, smiling for days as always, but flashes of her recent visit quickly
made Passion focus on what she was to learn this lifetime–she viewed her
time on earth differently now. She hadn't realized that until this moment.
Passion stopped for a second and checked her mind.

"There *is* no death." She paused in step and thought, "My kin is always
with me and–I am with them." Passion laughed and shook her head. "I
knew it all along, I was just afraid to think I could feel you
Justice–Mama–Daddy!"

She spoke to the wind, and then continued on her way. Each street
lamp seemed to sequentially light the way to her appointed destination,
which Passion was convinced, would be her old house–903 Powell Street.
She grinned childishly as she walked slowly and envisioned herself and her
little girlfriends: Debbie Ann, Cynthia, Valerie and Janice, sitting on her
porch, having one of their famous tea parties, their dolls all dressed up in
dresses each girl hand made herself. She briefly wondered how each one
was doing and vowed to call them when she got a chance.

She saw a young Justice Jr., as they used to call him, playing stickball in
the middle of the street that was never burdened with traffic. Other children were making scooters out of slats of wood taken from old, wooden
crates, they nailed the slats to the crates themselves along with old, steel
wheels from used roller skates. They adorned their scooters with paint and

bottle caps, bragged about which were the best, then raced down the block at top speed, completely disrupting the stickball game. The adults sat on the porches playing cards, sharing freshly baked delights and keeping their eyes on the "youngins'. Music was always coming from Papa Joe's house across the street. The Ink Spots or The Mills Brothers always greeted you when you stepped onto the 900 block of Powell Street.

The flickering porch light in front of 915 hypnotically lured her back into the spiritual realm. At first it attracted her curiosity, but then the incessant flickering made her feel as if she was dancing with a strobe light. She caught glances of herself moving in her last pose after she already had gone into a new one. Passion stopped herself; she was feeling weak in the knees and quite light-headed.

"Child, you look dazed. Won't you come sit up here on the porch a spell with your Auntie Jenny Mae?" Passion heard the old voice say.

"Auntie Jenny?" Passion said in astonishment, unable to fathom why the old woman would be outside this time of night, doing patchwork by a flickering lamppost. "Is that really you?"

"Of course it's me, I'm right here like I always been right here. Close your mouth. You look as shocked as you were the day they baptized you in Canarsie Bay. I remember it like it was yesterday. You were the cutest little thing, and you were scared to death. But you wanted to get baptized. We could always hear you singing louder than anyone else when we went to the water.

"Take me to da warrr duhh', take me to da warr duhhh," old Miss Jenny Mae chuckled as she imitated Passion when she was 4 years old. "Girl you loved that water. And look at you now...you looking all new like you done came out of some water."

Passion was rather radiant. Her experience on the mountaintop had elevated her spirit so she was shining like the moon. The big grin that spread across her face just then made her beam even more luminous.

"Keep that glow Passion. It's your gift, baby. Remember, just like God has given you Mama Lettie and Papa Joe to be your earthly parents, so he will give you another husband, and, another son....actually...a few more sons. So don't focus on who you don't have—they are always with you—focus on who you do have. You have an army. This whole village is up in arms over you and your Deuce. Shoot, a war done started. And a lot of people are gonna get hurt if you don't stop it. You got that warrior spirit girl; and you're not alone. 'Member what your daddy used to preach,

'...For we wrestle not against ourselves, but against powers and princi-palities in high places". Passion looked fearfully at the old woman as her voice changed and sounded just like Reverend Franklin's young voice echoed about her aura; it sounded just as it had 30 years ago.

"Go on now child. You best to be getting back to everybody. Just remember...I'm watching. He he heee. Me and everybody else. He he—heeee." Old Jenny Mae laughed and Passion, still seeing her as a child, but knowing she was a woman with a mighty task before her.

Passion could still hear her laughing, and found it strange and a little unnerving. She turned to say goodbye but her mother's long lost friend was gone. Then it dawned on Passion that she had been blessed from heaven once again. The woman she always called Auntie Jenny Mae had been buried 6 months before. She had died around Christmas, like a lot of folk seem to do. Passion had to sit down. Memories of going to the water with Auntie Jenny Mae began to flash before her eyes. That laugh of hers, and that beautiful singing voice.

"Take me to the *wa*-ter. Take me to the *wa*-ter. Take me to the *wa*-ter, to be baptized." Passion sat on the curb in front of 903 Powell Street singing, sobbing, and feeling like the chosen one. She thought about what Auntie

Jenny had said about a husband, and then she thought about what Justice had said about David. "They need to *stop.*," she said out loud, not caring if anyone knew she was sitting on the curb in the middle of the night, talking to herself. "And sons!–not one but sons! They need to *stop!*" she laughed out loud, imitating Auntie Jenny, "He he heeeee, he he heeee".

Her laughter abruptly ended as her own voice rang in her ears, "sons," "Oh God, where's Tres?" she almost panicked for a minute, but her spirit wouldn't allow her. It should be quite evident by now that you and yours are guided this night. You know Papa Joe has him. She was speaking calmly to herself, but her thoughts were racing flashing pictures of places they might have gone like a quick moving slide presentation. She stopped when the picture of Big Hip Hannah's Place was sharp and vivid before her. She started tracking through the same alleys and back yards Papa Joe had traveled through earlier with Tres literally following in his footsteps.

"Mama's coming, Tres, Mama's coming", she wanted to yell but instantly remembered that she had to keep a low profile, "Damn pigs are probably in my apartment right now', she thought in a whisper while envisioning her apartment. Passion was quite sure Mama Lettie, Connie or Anne had her children and was keeping them safe. She fought anger as she imagined pigs in blue sitting on her new couch with the African cover Papa Joe had given her when he returned from Ghana years ago. She pictured their flat footsteps leaving dirt throughout the apartment. "I'll have to clean every floor in the house." She spoke lowly to herself, quite perturbed since she and Justice never allowed anyone to come in their home with shoes on their feet. Passion remembered explaining it to Connie a few times, "Sister, just think of everything you must have stepped in on your way here–dirt, feces, urine, garbage–seen and unseen germs enough to keep us all sick. This is what you are allowing in your personal space. And besides that–you'll trudge all that crap through my clean, purified sanctuary. I love my home, Connie. This is where I eat, sleep and pray. No other place is more important for me to keep clean besides my internal temple. Which is why I am so particular about what I eat. We'll be complete vegetarians soon too. I've been hearing too many stories about what they do to the cows and chickens in this country." Connie was looking at her–sweetly stupefied as usual. Passion smiled to herself, Connie probably has the kids she concluded, assuring herself of their safety.

She was floating, but was quickly snatched back into 1963 as a screaming siren jarred her into reality. It was about a block away. So she nonchalantly slid into the nearest alleyway and walked between the shotgun houses and small lots of farmland that remained amongst the quickly developing community. Amazed at the sight of the much-believed promising future adjacent to the agricultural, painful past she decided that one was as scary as the other. Letting go of the little land they owned, too many had bought into the masked promises of the big city. Plantations verses projects. Which would be the worst?

Passion was asking herself these questions as she spied the nearby concrete and compared it to the dying daffodils lined up along her path. She could still hear the sirens. They were about two or three blocks away now, yet they seemed louder. Perhaps they were there all along. She was now taking notice of the flickering riot lights and the psychedelic effect they had on the houses, buildings and greenery. Although she was now fully conscious, she felt as if she was walking in a dream. Browns' Village was transformed, and somehow Passion knew it would never be the same.

She heard the el train and stopped to watch it pass. Passion had a thing about walking under the train as it was passing. As a child she was fearful of the bright orange sparks which fell fast from the rustling steel and wooden planks. The el also reminded her of her first childhood encounter with Big Hip Hannah. She laughed a little as she thought of the story she had told her boys when they got caught under the el. Miss Hannah had called Justice at the center one day, about three years earlier, to tell him she was holding Deuce and Tres hostage in the back of the bar 'cause she had caught them peeping in the side window and she "wasn't 'bout to lose her bidness over no kids". Passion made a closed-mouth, smirk-faced chuckle when she reminisced how afraid the boys looked when Justice brought them home to her. They were more afraid of one of her spankings than one of his. Justice never believed in hitting the children, he'd look at them and they would cry. Passion would look at them and they would laugh, so she'd end up spanking them mostly because they ticked her off. But this time she decided to tell them a story–before she punished them. She wanted them to know that she had broken her parents' rules before, and how she had suffered for it. She thought of the el when it was new, because it was, when Hannah first opened up. At first she didn't like the noisy el. Nobody did. Like the new high rises, it seemed to cast a shadowy darkness over the once bright, country-like community. Justice had brought the two then small boys to her bawling their eyes out. Passion thought of how shocked the boys looked when instead of yelling at them or grabbing the belt, she had calmly said, "You know what? I once did the same thing you did." The river of tears stopped instantly.

"It really is hard to resist going under the el huh? After all, that is where all the action is. Well, there was too much action under the el for me when I snuck over there,"

"You did Ma?" Deuce interrupted while Tres stood there in disbelief, his mouth hanging open.

"Yes I did. I was a little older than Tres myself, and I wasn't going to see no pretty ladies dancing dirty in the middle of the day. I went because everybody used to say that Miss Hannah smoked a cigar and beat up the biggest men in town. This–I wanted to see for myself. So. One day my Mama decided that I was old enough to go to the store by myself. And she sent me to the Jewish bakery to get her some pumpernickel bread. *Well*,"–Passion's "wells" were always let out in an exasperated sigh with drama deserving of an Emmy Award; her eyes got as big as saucers and her shoulders would be raised up high then dropped down drastically as the sigh escaped, " 2 blocks away from the bakery is Big Hip Hannah's Place, and you could hear the music, smell the food and imagine the good times

from that bakery come 5 o'clock, which is about the time that I was sent
to the store, because it was Friday and the bakery was about to close and
Mama wouldn't be able to get her bread until Sunday since the jews close
up on Saturday. I was told to run straight there. Well y'all, I ran all right,
but I ran straight to Big Hip Hannah's to see the cigar smoking, man-
whipping woman." The boys' eyes were fixed on Passion as if she was their
favorite TV show. They hung on every word smiling and shaking their little heads in disbelief.

"And, y'all won't ever guess what happened to me."

"What?!–WHAT?!"

"*Well,* I ended up drinking, fighting and being scared to death!"

"Go on Mama, you're pulling our leg."

"YEAH Ma, we ain't hardly gonna believe that!" Deuce chimed in,
looking at Tres for approval.

"I ain't telling nothing but the truth! Let me tell you what happened.
You see, I had nearly reached the front of Big Hannah's when I thought I
heard somebody following me. Actually, I thought it was your daddy. He
was always playing tricks on me, and following me whenever I didn't want
to be followed. So, I was so busy looking behind me, checking for Justice,
I didn't see what was coming towards me. *Well,* the very second I chose to
turn around, I was body-slammed to the ground by a grown man I never
saw before in my life."

Actually, Fat Back was tossing a rowdy drunkard out, as usual. He had-
n't seen little Passion tip-toeing up the street, practically below his knee
caps and ended up slamming the hundred fifty pound drunk right on top
of the child. BAM! The thrust of his heavy body caused her to fall flat on
her back and should've knocked her unconscious. She shocked the whole
bar, which was now outside attempting to pull the semi-conscious patron
off of her, but they had begun to roll down the uneven street.

"Boys, y'all should've seen your Mama. I couldn't believe this man had jumped me for my pumpernickel bread money. And–he wouldn't get off me either. Well, I started kicking and punching him as hard as I could. Next thing I know, we're rolling in the gutter. My favorite green and yellow dress was all torn and dirty, and I was furious. I was about to sock him with my double-fisted super jammie when Big Hip Hannah herself stepped in and broke up the fight."

The boys were rolling too. They laughed uncontrollably for about 5 minutes. Passion laughed too. She didn't realize they'd get such a kick out of her little story about disobedience.

They kept looking up at her; and every time they did, they 'd start laughing all over again. They'd laugh, then roll across the floor, pretending to be her rolling down the street. This went on for a few days until she grew tired of it as Tres recalled. It was the story about his Mom he chose to tell Miss Lucy. She was the one rolling now.

"Man I sure wish my Mama was here," Tres confided sadly.

Miss Lucy rubbed his shoulders, "Don't worry son, she's on her way. I just know it.

There was a long pause. Stress and sadness lingered between the two before Lucy could think of something helpful to say. Then she remembered how she would use her imagination to escape the cruelties of her reality. She would create her own scenario and it would always lessen the pain.

"I know what!" she said as gaily as she could. "Picture your mom fighting through the dark woods to get here. She's got herself a machete and a pistol–just like Harriet Tubman. And, she ain't taking nooo stuff! She's chopping down anything in her way 'cause she sees you and your sisters just like you were in front of her.

Tres tried not to laugh at the silly game Miss Lucy was playing, especially since she chose to act out the part of his mother. And she had this mean, but real goofy look on her face as she moved around the kitchen as she talked. After a minute he started seeing his mother dressed like a slave woman—tied up head, big plaid dress, too big shoes—swinging on everybody. The two cracked up laughing. They were laughing so hard; Papa Joe came out and just starred at them. He couldn't tell if they were crying or laughing from the high-pitched screams they were making. He told them he'd be out soon to tell them the plan. And they tried to wipe the grins off of their faces. But as soon as his back was turned, neither could contain the laughter they attempted to keep within.

Papa Joe was glad Tres wasn't falling apart anymore. He made a mental note to do something special for Miss Lucy.

"Tell me about your Papa Tres, if it's not too hard. I used to see him around all the time. But you tell me what you remember about him.

Before he spoke, Tres closed his eyes real tight and bit down on his bottom lip. His mind raced back to find the very best story about his dad that he could. Then he looked at Miss Lucy and smiled.

"INHERITANCE"—
"ODE TO THE BLACKMAN"

To be or not to be a Black man
is a decision you didn't dictate
God chose you especially for this honorable fate

He saw a need for strong hearts
made from strong seed
She saw the need for willingness
to love and to bleed
in the fight for fruit from the righteous tree
Warriors of love,
He chose you to be

To be or not to be a Black man
is a decision you didn't dictate
God chose you especially for this honorable fate

She saw a need for peace
in a world of quick triggers
He saw a need for Black people
not animals or "niggers"
to parent the world, nurture all needs
Warriors of love,
She chose you to be

To be or not to be a Black man
is a decision you didn't dictate
God chose you especially for this honorable fate

He saw the need for diversity
only a Black man could create
encompassing every color,
melanin designs what man creates
In Her image you've made everything,
through them you chose your mate

A Black man was the alpha,
the omega he'll be too
the world's a broken home, my brothers,
when it's lacking you
Justice is free for all
if you're healthy, right and true
Accept the inheritance and all your desires
will be given unto you.

C. Wright-Lewis 1/26/95

CHAPTER SEVEN

▼

"INHERITANCE"

BROWNS' VILLAGE
1961

Upon arriving home from Viet Nam, Justice viewed Browns' Village much differently than he had before. His heart was heavy and his spirit was weighted down from the horrors he had witnessed topped with his personal tragedy. The loss of his hand had actually saved him from being forced into savagery he deeply detested against his fellow man. As he sat in the dark foxhole amidst the sound of rapid gunfire and the sight of flares coloring the dark sky all sorts of colors, he was supposed to be listening to his orders the sergeant was bellowing. He wasn't really interested because he knew that this next mission was his. He knew it was his turn to burn a village, kill some women and children, and destroy his beliefs and morals. He didn't need to listen. He knew his job all too well. He watched the flares go up. Bright orange, red and yellowish gold. They reminded him of his children—the two boys he had left home to become a better provider. He secretly prayed neither would ever be a party to such cruelty and devastation. He smiled because he knew they would have loved the pretty rainbow painted against the night. He turned his deaf ear to the sergeant to pretend he was interested, but when he turned back around, a flare appeared to be coming right towards him, causing Justice to instinctively raise his right hand to deflect the object. The next thing he witnessed was his hand flying overhead as if it was jet propelled. He awoke in a hospital the next day. When he realized that he was still alive, he cried like a baby. Everyone thought he was in pain, or even in despair over losing his hand. But Justice was crying because he knew he was going home.

As his plane descended upon New York International Airport, soon to be Kennedy Airport, he looked down at Browns' Village—a brief 30 mile distant from the airport. He saw it all clearly as the plane appeared to move in slow motion above his beloved home. Justice vowed to himself and his God that he would protect his home, his village mosaic painted with every tint of brown, *his* Black paradise.

"Yeahh," Justice sighed as his exhaled from relief and exhaustion, "Thank God I'm home."

He was almost giddy as he watched his home from above. He saw the old, North Carolina- type row houses beyond the el train. He saw the new housing projects whose windows almost glistened in the sun's reflection. He also observed the motion of the freight trains, which ran beneath the el trains. For the first time in his life, he actually saw where they entered and exited Brooklyn.

"I wonder what's on those trains," he thought aloud with visions of military equipment flashing through his imagination, "they sure ain't running cattle and sheep through here anymore. Guess I need to find out," he had decided before he closed his eyes to allow the first tear to flow down his face since he lost his hand. He was anticipating Passion's reaction, and Papa Joe's reaction too. He envisioned salty tears simultaneously running into their mouths," I'm just glad to be alive", he practiced saying, "C'mon y'all–I'm home, I'm still alive, and that's all that counts." He managed a smiled while he imagined feeling their awaiting embraces. He predicted how they would all lock into one another's arms, holding so tight that on would think they would never let each other go. He could smell Passion's hair as he nuzzled her neck. The pilot's light voice disrupted his warming thoughts.

"Passengers would you please observe the seat belt signs. We are approaching our descent into Kennedy Airport. At this time, before we land, we would like to give a special welcome home to all our soldiers aboard. We thank you for risking your lives to preserve democracy all over the world. We're certain you killed as many communists as you could." Fellow passengers slapped Justice and other Viet Nam vets on their backs, or grinned at them from across the aisle while they buckled up, after the announcement. Justice politely returned their smiles, but offered no conversation. He was awaiting Passion.

Ironically, below the surface, the East Coast Express pulled into the freight yards adjacent to Kennedy Airport, and directly below the surface-leveled Long Island Railroad station. It was the mid point on the North Eastern line. This was the same line that used to run livestock from the south to the northern cities and continuously stocked Atlantic Avenue slaughterhouses. Its giant, refrigerated boxcars stored every kind of commodity, from every kind of company or corporation across the eastern border of the United States. It stopped at several, small towns and big cities along the east coast and traded at coordinated points with other freights which ran further south, south west, north west and just west. Its well-kept, shiny-steel tracks were popular and envied by every other line in the country. Its up-keep was consistently maintained by any prisoner of the state–doing time. Chain gangs made the East Coast Express' route the fastest and most efficient railroad line in the country. Its top-of-the-line binary engine was unsurpassed in its day, but since 1945 its replacement, a Corliss engine encased in metallic silver had a notorious reputation in the business. It had broken a record and delivered shipments across country in such a short amount of time, it gave competition to the wildcat locomotives that carried mail only, and therefore used only one car. The East Coast Express whizzed back and forth through the south and the north delivering all the wants and needs of the masses. Now that cattle were fewer, military merchandise–some marked nuclear, and drugs practically monopolized the colorful cars. They traveled sandwiched between the produce and apparel-filled cars- eight runs every twenty-four hours, three hundred and sixty five days a year.

Pit stops in every state from Banestown in Miama to Brooklyn's Canarsie Bay, across the border from Browns' Village, became very popular for the smaller communities surrounding them. They availed small marketplaces throughout the big cities, providing a new trade along every old Native American trail from Miami to Canada. The new trade had begun to be quite a feasible commodity; the dry, white, crystalline, bitter powder, derived from morphine, a popular drug, derived from the poppy plant widely used "medicinally" in Viet Nam on wounded soldiers. It was call "horse," "smack," "white lightning," "kicks," and "the white lady." The "white lady" rode upon the "Iron horse" and stopped to meet everyone she could along the line. The station she disembarked in Canarsie Bay was the same station Fat Back and Brother made their big deals on imported goods: top grade beef and pork, cigarettes, top shelf liquor, marijuana; gold and freshly dried, pure cocaine and the increasingly popular "white lady" by the kilo.

A combination of shell shock and the loss of his hand caused Justice memory losses. He had forgotten about the many times his father had taken him to watch the trains in Canarsie Bay, and how much Justice loved to watch them pass. He was always proud to see the colored men working on the train; he was too young to realize how they were being treated.

"I'm a be a trainman Daddy," he would always say to Papa Joe.

"Don't you remember?" asked Papa Joe after he and his only son had settled into a conversation about war and coming home. He had told Papa Joe what he had observed from the plane and asked what these trains carry back and forth.

"I'd like to know that myself. Based on the changing behavior of some of young people, especially boys like yourself, coming home from the war, I would imagine all kinds of drugs and illegal contraband. You know some of those crooked union boys are on the other side of this."

"You're probably right," Justice had thought, unable to come up with anything else at the time.

Papa Joe knew Justice appeared to readjust to being back in the big city, but like most vets, he was having nightmares. He consistently dreamt of running through a giant rice paddy, holding a young Vietnamese child. He could see the child's mother on the opposite end of the field beckoning to him to bring her child across. The field is soggy and he slips every few steps. Finally he slides and falls. But when he falls the grenade that the child was concealing rolls out of the child's pants. The child is rolling away from him in slow motion. Crying for Justice. But before Justice can grab the small boy, the child rolls right into a mine and blows up right in front of Justice's face. The child's body parts sail through the air. Justice raises his hand to protect his face when his hand breaks off and flies through the air with the others. His screams awakened the children and Mama Lettie next door. They knew it was 3:00 in the morning.

Justice's nightmare's had gotten him into the habit of rising, bathing, and being fully dressed at 4 a.m. He could never sleep much after the daily 3 a.m. shock. He'd go to the kitchen, turn on his transistor radio and listen to WWRL (the only colored radio station in New York City), hoping, "*you-oo-oo-oo send me*" would be next, as he watched the workers heading towards the factory further up Sutter Avenue. The stillness usually bothered him. It reminded Justice of the tranquility of Saigon's mornings, just before an ambush. He was still trying to figure out how they always knew his whereabouts. The native in Justice taught him to listen to the ground, watch the stars and travel in the right direction, even without a compass, but Charlie almost always sought him out. They called the Vietnamese enemy "Charlie," but Justice never knew why. He guessed it dehumanized the people enough to make them deserving objects of enmity.

"Damn!" he almost yelled angrily. "Where the *fuck* were you hiding Charlie?"

Drawing nearer, Justice heard the rumbling crescendo of a freight train pulling into the nearby station. Its sound was very different from the el train that ran two blocks away. "Naw," Justice told himself, "that was a freight–moving below us, where we can't see it. All the time. Is that where you were Charlie–below us–in tunnels perhaps? Watching me in the day, then sneaking up on my ass at night?–Below us.–Yeah. Uh-huh.–I bet that's it.–Just like them damn freight trains. What's on those suckers anyway? Charlie. Sneaking up on my ass in the middle of the night. You ain't taking me here. Justice is home god dammit! Justice is home."

It was 5 a.m., and the crack of an early summer morn. Justice was scared to death by another nightmare, and everyone had gone back to sleep as usual–except him. He made his usual cup of coffee, turned to "RL" and headed towards his window. But this day, when the train whistle blew, Justice answered. A brief 15 minutes later, he found himself standing on Junius Street, starring into the freight yards on Dumont and Livonia Avenues. A briefer 5 minutes after that, he was down inside of the train yard, sitting on the hill, curiously spying the empty freight that sat on the side of the yard–away from the tracks.

The new weekly spillage, lay upon the freight yard, with a railroad caboose, filled with hairbrushes of every possible style and size. The brushes were everywhere. The caboose lay overturned. They often didn't make the turn at Livonia en route to the last stop on the East Coast Express line–Canarsie Bay. And all sorts of merchandise was available on a weekly basis–some worth nothing, like broomsticks or shelf brackets, and other times t-shirts, bathroom rugs, window cleaner–useful five-and-dime items. Sometimes the spillage created a nuisance. Especially when the children got into the freight yard, removed items and spread them all over the neighborhood. Once, ice cream Popsicle sticks were everywhere–parks, bus stations, on the curb. Soon after, every Arts& Crafts class in the community was constructing log cabins with Popsicle sticks.

This week's gift to Browns' Village was every hue and hint of color paint within a sealed can could have. Justice couldn't "let *all* that paint go to waste", he repeated every time someone asked where had gotten the paint. He had begun picking up cans after his third morning of visiting the yards. It was about 5 a.m., and as he was bending over to pick a can up, he heard light footsteps uphill, about ten yards away. At first he thought the police or some sort of security officer was stalking him. But then he heard their voices and some of their conversation. He automatically knew they were either crooked cops or mob gangsters because they were talking about the weight of the new shipment and the quickest way to distribute it before the end of the week. He also knew they were colored because of one's heavy southern drawl.

He stood as still as a deer frozen in flight, standing amongst the tossed purple paint cans covering the grassy tracks. He planned to pretend he couldn't see nor hear them, and to begin clanging paint cans together, hoping the illusion would make his presence an unimportant coincidence they'd overlook. But the other one began to speak with a most familiar voice.

"What's brother doing hanging out with Country." Justice had heard of Fat Back, but had never met him before. He decided to call Brother instead. Justice knew Brother's entire family, but he didn't know of the new lifestyle Brother acquired while Justice was in Viet Nam.

"Hey Brother! Is that you man?"
"Wow!–Hey it's Justice!"

Brother ran to Justice, forgetting himself, his new job and his new image. Justice moved towards Brother as well. The four out-stretched, black arms depicted the genuine love for one another the children in Browns' Village had grown up having for one another. Justice pictured Brother as the little boy remembered. He was about five years older than Brother and always saw him as a kid. Justice's large 6 ft. 4–200 pound frame overshadowed Brother's 5 ft. 11- 165 pounds and lifted him up in the air like was still a little kid. Brother laughed like a little kid too. The picture-perfect scene of two brothers greeting in the rising sun sickened Fat Back.

"Fat Back–this is my man Justice. He just came back from the jungle, man.

But Fat Back was disturbed and annoyed by Justice's presence.
"What you doin' here?–What you looking fo'"
"You own the freight yards?–What's your name brother?"
"You ain't none of my kin"
"I'm taking some of this paint. I'll see you around brother; you got a nice friend", Justice was walking backwards as he talked, looking Fat Back dead in the eyes. He looked him up and down, turned, then walked away.

He could hear Brother explaining, "He just got home–that's my homes."

Justice was letting his hair grow. He called it a "bush." And he was wearing dungarees and a long, toga-like shirt called a dashiki. His eyes were riveting because they appeared to have a gray circle around the pupils, giving them a sense of depth. So seeing him for the first time usually did take one aback. And, he did only have one hand.

"What kind of nigger is that?—What's his game?"
"You don't understand Justice, man. Justice is cool. He's deep."
"Well he needs to keep his deep ass out of this yard. You tell him that."

Passion passed Justice the word on Brother when he went back home. Even his parents were against him now, she had explained. " He and Fat Back not only sold drugs, but they burglarized people's homes. Everybody figures they're both using the drug as well since they'd gone into stealing. They're working for somebody. But I don't think Big Hannah knows anything about it. She still doesn't allow drugs in her place and Fat Back and Brother are spending less and less time there.

"This heroin is a real problem Justice and somebody's just pumping it into our neighborhood."
"Passion, you know I'm on this. The brothers will deal with Brother. In the meantime, let's put this paint to good use. I've got an idea."
Without a warning, murals were being painted everywhere. Empty, cold, brick city walls once requesting, "Post No Bills," now portrayed images of every African king and queen imaginable.
Nefertitti adorned the front of 414 Sutter, King Hatshepsut and Queen Nzinga faced one another on the Blake Avenue side. And up on Stone Avenue Imhotep and Ramses IV reigned. Other buildings wore the faces of Tutkahankton, Shaka Zulu, Nat Turner, Sojourner Truth, Harriet Tubman, Ida B. Wells, Booker T. Washington, W.E.B. Dubois and all of his partners in the war for freedom marched across on the village walls

followed by the words: "From Up From Slavery" – to–" Brownsville, Never Ran, Never Will!" Beautiful shades of brown skin adorned in painted red, green and gold African crowns and gowns were all one giant inspiring mosaic of African history of the Motherland and its bastardized American brother land. On the front of the community center, Justice himself had painted an African village only an African could fathom. Jungle tree green hung down in leaves and swayed in the grass, joyous divine blue skies met with the teal ocean's white-curled waves, caramel, milk chocolate and cocoa colored bodies danced to dashing drummers on the right, and on the left merchants sold their man-made wares, creatively positioned atop the red, rich African soil. Justice had painted huts any urban architect would have loved to design; some had sloped roofs, patio decks and extravagant awnings made of wood and straw. The scene caused people to begin to stop and stand in front of the center in amazement. To further entertain the people, and draw them near, Justice began to play records of African or Afro-Cuban bands. He attached them to his speakers and played them loud enough for a passerby to hear. The brothers in the community had organized committees from the three buildings in each courtyard of the apartment complex and they were all working wonders, but Justice had just astonished the entire community. The spirit of the music and the magic of the art lured the angelic ancestors whose job it was to protect the community, and in return they inspired Justice to play his old drum–despite his missing hand. He had painted a one-handed djembe drummer within his mural and everyone automatically expected to meet and witness the wonderful man who played with a hand, a nub and all his heart.

Once the project was completed, Mr. White, the Chief of Grounds and Tenant's Affair's asked Justice to become Program Director. Justice accepted. He had been impressed with Justice from the moment he introduced himself as "a concerned, lover of my community, who wants to make things better." Justice had worn his uniform when he went to meet Mr. White, knowing he'd impress him. He had promised that the paint job wouldn't cost Mr. White a dime, and it hadn't. Mr. White had found a gold mine in Justice. A major part of his job was to relate to the tenants and act as a liaison between the city executives and the tenants, but couldn't reach the people. In meetings, he had promised after-school programs, free breakfast and lunch programs in the summer, a nursery, and a Summer Day Camp. But many of the former southerners had past encounters with the K. K .K. and hate-filled racist whites, and didn't trust a white face—no matter how much it smiled or what it offered. But no one ever went to the center.

Justice had his own plans. And they went into action the moment the people responded to the call of the drum. Justice knew there were more drummers around because Papa Joe had taught a drum class for years when Justice and his friends were 8 years old. Many of them hadn't picked up a drum since they were about eleven or twelve, but hearing Justice made them remember the feeling they used to get when they played as children. It was a powerful feeling. Once one's hands had become one with the drum, it was as if a spirit would take over and play with your hands. Hands would move without being told by the young brains. Hearing their own rhythm, they would magically move over the djembe, allowing the awesome instrument to speak. One by one, the memories of little boys, now in their twenties, drove them to The Umoja Community Center, and on Friday night, they jammed.

The Sutter Avenue Community Center quickly became the place to be for children, youth and adults. With Passion as his partner and Papa Joe giving eldership blessings and support, Justice couldn't go wrong. They created, "The Umoja Nursery and Day Care Center", "The Umoja After-School and Summer Program" and "The Umoja Reading Programs: for adults and children; children not only received help with homework, participated in intramural sports, and took classes in crafts, martial arts, sewing, cooking, craft building, quilting, music theory and an increasingly famous drum class taught by Justice. So many had signed up for Justice's class that he had to create 3 different classes—one for the children, one for the teens and one for adults. The males attempted to protest girls and women taking the drum classes, but Justice tolerated no discrimination. "If I can play with one hand, I'm sure she can play with two," was always his response to anyone's complaint. And it seemed to work. If they wanted to play with Justice, they had to be fair.

The sisters were astounding, and Justice's pride–partially because the odds were against them. But mostly because Passion had instilled something in his heart that made him forever passionate and understanding of those whose rights were stolen in any capacity. On the night he had come home from completing the last mural at the community center, he was bursting with joy because Mr. White had offered to make him director. But Justice's heart was troubled because no one but his family knew about his nightmares and flashbacks, his anger against the government for subjecting him and so many others they were subjecting everyday to the evils of unnecessary warfare. He wasn't even sure if he should be working so close to people so soon after coming home.

"Baby, do you think I'm ready to fight in another war? I'm still seeing burning babies in my sleep."

"But that's exactly why you should Justice. Those babies won't leave until you can replace those memories with something more positive. I think this is a great opportunity for you to do exactly that. Besides, I'm gonna help." Her big smile made him smile too. "I see it like this Justice. You have the power of the victim."

"Power of the victim? See girl, now you making stuff up." Justice was beginning to laugh, but when he looked into Passion's innocent eyes, he could see that she was serious.

"Yes Justice, I'm dead serious. I see you as a victim *and* we've *all* been fighting in a war all our lives just because we're colored and just because we're here.

"I know that baby."

"I know you know that. So look at this. I think that you are receiving this opportunity from God because it is not just an opportunity to work and get healthier, but it's an opportunity to let the community know, what you know. You are the one who is supposed to hip the brothers and sisters in our community to what's going on in the world. 'Cause they don't know. Then maybe we can have some control over our children's education, and teach more of our history and culture like Daddy always said. C'mon Justice, the next move is yours, so you can change the game.

"You think I can do all that huh? Passion was sitting in his lap at this point, but his head lay on her breast. He was rubbing her belly, which held their second daughter, though they didn't know that yet. "You just love me, that's all. That's why you think I'm so great," he whispered before they kissed.

"That's right. I love you Justice, and I know you can do anything. You made it out of that jungle baby. You came home to us for a reason. And, I'm so glad you're here."

"I love you too Passion", he whispered even softer as they lay listening to the low train rumblings from below, and then above the surface, serving as a mantra to Justice, causing him to meditate deeply within Passion and himself as well. The rhythm of the trains sounded like drums being caressed by the light hands of a woman. His heart began to beat in the same manner. He and Passion moved like-wise. Her spirit seemed to spiral about his person—her energy electrically charging him. His spirit responded, unable to be contained as the rumbling mellowed into a hum that sent him deep into the darkness that preceded the brightness of revelation's light. Their passion was still there. It hadn't faded a bit. They slithered up, down and around one another's bodies as if each one was lubricated with hot oils. It was their natural flow at work. There could be no other Passion for Justice, nor no other Justice for Passion. They had been wed a hundred times before, lifetime after lifetime after lifetime. Their oneness was so spiritual that they glowed in the dark at the height of their ecstasy, and found it necessary to beckon their spirits back to the earth realm once their bodies had landed from the galactic ride.

They talked all night that night–writing and planning the mission of the Umoja Community Center. So whenever Justice heard the sisters drumming, he thought of that night; the sisters could drum all day for Justice.

Passion was the nursery and day care provider, with the help of Mama Lettie and several other sisters who had babies of their own. They used the day care on a part-time basis and worked there part-time as well to help other sisters out. Each sister served and was served. Many of them found it a relief to just come to the center whether they needed help or not. So many of their husbands were at war or waiting to go, they began gathering in discussion groups to preoccupy themselves. Seeing what the war had done to Justice made everyone uneasy and distrustful of the government. Listening to the teachings of a young Muslim minister from Uptown called Malcolm X, and the increasing protests against discrimination and brutality across the country caused songs of faith, protest, God and war to spill out of the windows of "the center" into the streets of Browns' Village and its neighboring communities. The people of the community were becoming conscious and it showed in the way they dressed, the way they walked and the way they talked. Common conversation was almost always political, which was exactly what Justice wanted.

Cultural exchanges occurred during holidays and seasonal festivals in a way that they never had before. Sharing of information rediscovered since and before the Harlem Renaissance was discussed. History from indigenous people who hadn't lost the ways of the elders and ancestors were reintegrated into the lifestyle of the new inner-city American African natives. Words of Negro baseball leagues, the Tuskegee Airmen, Booker T. Washington, W.E.B. Dubois, Ida B.Wells and Sojourner Truth, Charles Houston and his student–Thurgood Marshall, David Walker, Nat Turner and Harriet Tubman had always been honored in the community, but now, the spirits of Shaka Zulu, Queen Nzinga, Imhotep, and Queen of Sheba had re-evolved. The people loved to hear of African greatness through stories they had never heard before. Uprisings and escapes had been the pride-filled sagas they told. The children and adults danced in beautifully painted green, red and gold African garb, while women and men drummers kept the back beat, syncopated rhythms in 2/4 or 6/8 time. Everyone sang and told African folklore taught to them by ancestors and ancestors of friends and neighbors. Everyone cooked and shared different Pan-African dishes from around the world, then listen to the community leaders speak. Justice had become a favorite among these community leaders. His height and charisma gave him presence. His hand always caught one's attention, if they hadn't noticed him. His eyes always compelled one to look into them, but it was his melodic, baritone voice that retained the attention of even those who had no intention of listening. His voice was stirring and passionate. His message was insightful and uplifting. And since he had returned home, Justice would always speak about the same two things which concerned everyone else: repercussions of the Viet Nam War and the influx of illegal narcotics into the community.

The longer Justice was home, the more he was driven to the freight yards and the more he was being driven to find out why more and more brothers were winding up strung out on heroin. They would come to the Umoja Center two or more days after shooting up, destitute and desperate. They always wanted to end the addiction, and realized they, "had monkeys on their backs" as everyone would say. But in actuality, surviving the withdrawal process was something none of them could visualize themselves doing. They had seen horrors and heard rumors of convulsions, heart attacks and paralysis. Justice wanted to help them, but wasn't quite sure just yet. One thing he knew for sure was, once he had run into Brother and Fat Back that morning and overheard their conversation, he knew who the war was against. He knew Passion had been correct. And, he knew he had to change the game.

Although they met as a community every week, the brothers had their night to meet and so did the sisters. Both groups discussed the very same topics, but their solutions varied greatly. The sisterhood discussed creating a clinic, organizing everyone who had taken nursing classes or was interested in doing so. They also decided to call on elders like Mama Lettie who was cognizant of herbal remedies for cleansing the circulatory system. But at the Brotherhood meeting, the brothers had decided that they would confront Brother and firmly coerce him into taking them to Fat Back, whom they would coerce into revealing his connection, then permanently run him out of town.

Fat Back was not known as an accessible or a receptive brother. And, all anyone knew of him was rumored until Justice was an eyewitness to Fat Back's dirty deeds and carelessly arrogant attitude. He was big enough to whip anybody he wanted, so no one was exactly trying to get in his way. But he wasn't bigger than Justice.

"I ain't down with killing a brother. But if he's hurting the community, that's different." One brother shouted.

"That's right! This is different from running numbers or bootleg liquor. This is a drug that kills. That's all it does is kills!" Justice was ranting; his emotions causing others to scream out.

"Let's storm Big Hip Hannah's!"

"Let's take it down!"

"Hold on now. Hold on now. We have to plan this right. We ain't no mob. We don't ever want to destroy any part of our own community, but we will pay this brother a visit."

And they all agreed with Justice.

Five brothers, all Viet Nam veterans aiding Justice, seized Brother the next night about 4 a.m. They were waiting inside of his tenement flat when he came home. They slipped up on him from behind the second he walked into the door, draped a pillowcase over his head, punched him in the head, kicked him in the groin, and carried him out. Blood appeared on the pillowcase, but his low murmurings let them know he was all right.

They took him to the community center and tied him to a chair in the back room while they waited for Justice.

"We should kill him right now. Then we get the other one, and kill him too. End of problem," other young, angry brothers nodded in agreement.

"Robbing people, now killing people—and we call you brother?"

"Shut-up y'all, or I won't be able to wait for Justice."

"Justice is *here*," his voice was deep, firm and concentrated. It stilled all movement. Interrupted every thought. His eyes scanned the room intently and peered sharply into all ten. He snatched the pillowcase off of Brother's head and lifted it up by pushing his index finger under the tip of Brother's chin.

"What's shaking Brother? Come on, open your eyes baby. Don't be afraid."

"I didn't hurt your family Justice. I wouldn't hurt you ... you, you, you my man." Brother was shaking so fiercely, his lip was quivering against the rhythm of his body.

Justice rolled Brother's sleeves up and observed the needle marks from his wrist to his inner forearm—some cracked, infected and puss-filled.

"If you know you're sick, why don't you go to the hospital?"

"I can't afford no hospital Justice. So won't you just let me go? You know, you know I ain't responsible for nothing. It's this white lady now—she be doing things to me. Let me go Justice. You don't want to fuck around with Fat Back; he's a dangerous man. I told him you're coo–coo- cool."

"Where *is* Fat Back, Brother? Tell us where he is right now or we'll help you dry out *Cold Turkey* style."

"I'll die Justice. Don't do that to me brother. I'm still *Brother*. You can't just kill me."

"Man, you don't care about nobody but yourself. So don't try to con me Brother. I don't believe a damn word you say. So we're gonna leave you right here until we make a believer out of you. Say amen."

Justice and the five brothers walked out after they locked the windows and the door. One brother kept watch outside the door to help Brother to the bathroom and get help when he started getting sick.

Brother was strong until about 10:00 that morning–his usual fix time. First, his nose started running, and then the scratching began. He rocked and scratched so violently, he caused his arms to bleed. Delirious with pain he twisted, turned and contorted his body until he almost got himself loose.

"JUSTICE! *JUSTICE!!–JUST-US, JUST–-US!!!*" his screams were heard at the front of the community center, causing people to question.

The brothers quickly broke in, gagged him and gave him new linen and water until Justice arrived. Brother refused the water or any food they offered him. He was too sick to eat. Justice had to help Passion at home because she had just delivered their fourth child–another girl. Now they had Justice, Deuce -, Mecca and little Zaire. All of the brothers were congratulating Justice, but kept their energy focused on Brother.

"I think Brother's ready to talk to me today. What's happening–*Brother*?"

"Fat Back lives on Osborne Street, man. 292 Osborne Street. Last room on the first floor." He was sweating profusely and whining instead of talking. But it didn't faze Justice at all. Justice pulled out a little foil packet and teasingly hung it in front of Brother's face.

"Naw Brother, we want you to escort us. You show us the secret entrance, then you can have your little fix."

They waited until midnight, when Brother knew Fat Back would be arriving home. Then they left. Brother was bent over, exaggerating the pain in his stomach. He was faking and they knew it. They expected him to try and break loose and he did. The second they stepped out of the back door, Brother snatched the empty foil packet out of Justice's hand and ran as fast as he could, up the ramp and into the courtyard of the Blake Avenue buildings. The brothers had him surrounded at that point. They wrestled him down to the ground, but once they had grabbed him and began to rise, the cops were on them like white on rice. A concerned neighbor had reported violent, blood-curdling screams for help coming from the courtyard.

They let Brother go and took the brothers to the precinct. Brother had said that he wanted to press charges, but everyone knew better. The cops knew that Brother was a junkie once they heard him speak. And, they knew that he wouldn't be coming to press charges in the morning. So they took the brothers to the precinct just to flex their muscles a little. But Justice wouldn't stand for it. He demanded his phone call and recited his rights loudly and consistently for so long they gave it to him. Papa Joe came down and bailed them all out before the night was over. But it was too late. Brother had gotten to Fat Back, gotten his fix and the two had planned their counterattack.

Justice couldn't sleep once he had gotten home. Passion greeted him at the door. She hadn't slept either.

"You better watch your back now Justice", she warned before she laid down with him to help relieve him of the stress, "you can't trust Brother".

She fell asleep with the baby about 7 a.m. and the apartment was peaceful and still. Justice stood before the window and thought about the new plan he and the brothers must now execute. And, he decided to go see his father. He knew Papa Joe would be awake at this time, so he bathed, dressed and headed out of the door. Passion's aura was still all over him. He doubled back to kiss his Passion, the new baby and all of his children. He stood for a moment and wept silently as he watched them all sleep. He was so glad to be home to protect them. His boys were getting so strong and mature. Tres was now nine years old and Deuce was going on eight. They were fine little warriors, he thought. Justice knew it was his mission to destroy this plan of whoever was in control to flood Browns' Village with drugs and he wouldn't rest until the job was done.

He placed a red, black and green kufi Passion had knitted for him on his short Afro and descended the back staircase. It led out to Powell Street, which was 3 short blocks to Papa Joe's house on Livonia. But the second Justice stepped on the bottom stair, Fat Back jumped in front of him, standing a mere inch above him and breathing hard through his flaring nostrils into Justice's face. Justice tried to maintain his cool and slyly reach in the small of his back for his piece. He quickly changed his mind when he felt Brother approaching him from behind.

"You should've killed me when you had a chance Justice."

"I guess you're right–*Brother*," Justice said coolly.

"I told you I didn't like this strange *nigger*, Brother. It's gon' be my pleasure to take your ass to lunch–*nig-ger*.

"You gonna kill me Brother? You gonna take my babies' daddy away? You gonna destroy the community that loved you Brother? Are gonna break your mother's heart even more by killing me–Brother? Even if this man kills me, it will be your fault. You gonna take care of my family for me? You gonna look out for Papa Joe? He looked out for you when you were a kid." Justice had spoken so rapidly, it confused Brother for a minute. But Fat Back touched Brother's back, and made the choke sign with his left hand and Brother knew what he had to do.

"Well I ain't no kid no more. And, you were right last night Justice. I don't care about nobody but me, except maybe the white lady."

Brother grabbed the gun from Justice's backside.

"I don't need your Papa Joe, except to maybe rob here every other week." He and Fat Back were laughing. And Fat Back now had his forearm and elbow stuck in Justice's neck. "I don't need you. And, I ain't your *brother, the name is Paul.*" Brother raised the gun to Justice's head and shot him right in the temple to ensure his demise. Fat Back grabbed the piece and shot Justice again in the front of his forehead. Then the two fled.

All of Browns' Village mourned. They hailed Justice's spirit as if it was the spirit of a king. The brothers vowed to kill Fat Back and Brother, but the two seemed to have disappeared.

Tres' fondest memories of Justice were those of Justice painting the center and playing the djembe drum with one hand, he told Miss Lucy. But what she remembered most vividly was being outside of the building when Passion got the news. Everyone in and outside the building heard Passion holler. Her uncontrollable, pain-filled wails brought everyone in earshot to their knees.

All of Browns' Village mourned. They hailed Justice's spirit as if it was the spirit of a king. Hundreds came to give honor to Justice. They came from thousands of miles—musicians, family and social activists who knew what Justice stood for and respected his passion for his people. The funeral stopped traffic in Brooklyn, commanding a dignitary's salute from every uniformed civil servant. Sadly, Papa Joe was distraught and seemingly destroyed. Passion kept a regal appearance, but broke down repeatedly with the family. The children were shattered. The community was devastated. People mourned and memorialized until they didn't know what else to do. Once The Umoja Community Center was renamed The Justice Freeman Community Center folks began to realize Browns' Village had lost Justice forever. The mural depicting his essence now had candles about his feet, and white lights encircling him. Justice would not be forgotten.

The brothers continued to meet. Papa Joe was their new leader. They vowed to kill Fat Back and Brother, but the two had disappeared that same morning. They had intentionally got themselves arrested. Seconds after they murdered Justice, the police were arresting them for causing a disturbance in the train station. And being junkies with smack still in their possession, they got a little time in Brooklyn's Detention House. In a month they were free. Brother stayed in Queens until he heard that many of the brothers were drafted or were spending a lot of time uptown with Minister

Malcolm X. He eased back into Browns' Village in less than a year. Fat Back had gone south until he heard that things had calmed down too. Big Hip Hannah wouldn't allow him to work for her unless he was clean. He swore he was, but his stay with her was brief.

The two worked out of an abandoned building near the freight yard. Every junkie knew where to find them.

"RETRIBUTION"

Coming around after
going around
Ten-fold–PREPARE
Should've prayed to God
that it wouldn't go there

Inflicted by your own curses
what's worse is
you still can't see
because you oppress another,
You can't be free

The drug you pushed
is now pushing you
white junkies–black honkies
Plantation and zoo
Maintenance is high up on the avenue

Feel the poison flow thru your vain
the loss of power
precedes the pain

Live the irony of it all
'cause without it
you're doomed to fall
to the depths of the Hell
you have created,
the good and the bad all have waited

to witness the day
retribution was slated.

In the madness, that made the maim
you leave this world just like you came
Carrying baggage that's filled with sin
what goes around
comes around again.

C. Wright-Lewis 8/5/99

CHAPTER EIGHT

"RETRIBUTION"

BROWNS' VILLAGE
July 18, 1963
Just after midnight

From four short blocks away, Passion saw the dim light coming from Big Hip Hannah's. It was apparent the place was closed, but Passion knew someone was there. She kept checking behind herself, listening for footsteps or deep breathing. She looked around every corner before turning, often slapping her back flat against the hot bricks like a spy. After peering down the well-lit, empty street, she made a move in and out of the light, then tip-toed back into the darkness across the avenue, closer to the el.

Looking back for black and white police cars, she picked up what she thought was David Walker's silhouette walking with another man, but the man with him appeared to be limping. She decided it wasn't him and continued walking gingerly toward Big Hannah's, staying away from street and riot lights, dodging behind buildings and through alleyways.

Passion was mistaken. It *was* David; and the limping man was the being-dragged, much sought-after Brother. And the man walking in front of him, who Passion hadn't seen, who caused him to limp, was the tall afro—Malik. If Malik had had five more minutes alone with Brother, Brother would have been dead. Luckily, David caught Malik right before he inserted an overdose of heroin into Brother's main artery.

He had ascended a rooftop himself. He had seen Malik from the building he stood upon which was on the corner of Sutter and Stone. From there he followed Malik, knowing what he had in mind. David had also spotted Brother from the rooftop and watched him stumble from Rockaway Avenue to Stone Avenue and Sutter and then slip into the backdoor of a store fortunate enough to still be standing. He was still high from his last fix, but his head was becoming too clear now and he didn't want to think about all that had happened. Justice was haunting him.

David had sent the word out amongst the brothers, so Afros were hidden about the vicinity where Brother was expected to show. They hid within the midst of crowds, behind opened doors of burned buildings and inside the bottom of staircase exits waiting for retribution. Malik stood stiffly behind his chosen exit door. He was invisible and stiff as stone, but was concerned that the sound of his heart would reveal his position in the dank stairwell basement where the light bulb he had broken lay shattered all over the floor.

Malik's hands were itching. They were red and hot from the chemical particles that rubbed off as he had lit each of his man-made dynamite sticks. He knew he had lost control long ago. At this point he didn't care.

He had blown up half of the stores of his beloved community—stores he couldn't wait to see when he knew he was returning home from 'Nam. His rage had thrust upwards in balls of fire from rooftops along Sutter Avenue, and it still was not enough.

"Brother must die," he replied to himself, "that's the only thing that would make it better," wondering what would suffice in calming his heart.

Malik breathed deeply, attempting to slow his heart rate and fine-tune his focus. He hummed deeply, repeating a mantra taught to him by a yogi he had met in Greenwich Village in the city. It usually tranquilized him after an episode of flashbacks and made him civil. The best it did for him tonight was to make him still enough not to blow his cover when he heard Brother tripping down the stairs hoping to down enough of the pint of Smirnoff he had bought from the bootlegger to help him sleep until he could cop some more smack in the morning. He had torn the bottle cap off 30 seconds after leaving the boot's back door behind the fish market on Belmont Avenue and succeeded in choking himself when he tried to chug the vodka down his throat like it was water. He had an edge and he knew he had to calm it or he'd be sick for the rest of the night.

Brother lay in the grass a few feet from the market place in one of the few remnants of rural Brooklyn left—a plot of land between a row of houses and the market place. It was covered with grass and the remains of a recent revival tent was scattered about the land. He heard no one or no thing until a few rats ran pass, not even acknowledging his presence. His head spun as he looked down at himself. He decided that this was the end of his life, and that he would remain a junkie until he died.

Police cars patrolling the area startled him out of a deep nod and convinced him to scurry like the rats, into a safe haven. That's when Brother remembered his old stairwell. It had been his favorite because the people who lived there rarely used it. When he was strung out, it was his private apartment. Even Fat Back didn't even know about it. Malik knew about it though. And so did David. They knew every hideout. Brother began to move towards his hiding place. He never looked over his shoulder, nor

wondered if anyone was watching him. He was tired now, woozy and nau-
seous. He slipped into the doorway, jimmied the lock, and then half fell
down the staircase leading to ambush. As Brother landed on the last step,
Malik inhaled as much of the stale air as he could through his nostrils. The
deep breath made his body become erect and his aural abilities sharpen.
The second Brother staggered through the door marked exit, Malik
stepped from behind the door, slipped behind Brother and put him in a
chokehold. Malik violently landed on top of Brother after forcing him to
the floor. He tied Brother's hands behind his back and punched him in his
temple so hard, Brother momentarily lost consciousness. Malik threw the
junkie's body in the corner and began to unwrap the foil packet he had
brought to send Brother on his last fling with the white lady. He cooked
the poison quickly and filled the needle. Just as the tip of the needle had
entered Brother's skin, David stepped into the doorway.

"Drop the needle Malik...DROP IT!" he shouted loud enough to
shake the both of them out of their strange states. "Come on baby—pull it
out and drop it. We need this brother alive. Can you hear me Malik? For
our plan to succeed we *need* Brother,".

He paused a moment, unsure of what Malik would do next. He stood
aside of Brother's horizontal body, but moved in closer and closer until his
eyes and Malik's eyes were fixed upon each other. Malik shook his head
and waved, as if he was being annoyed by a fly, then David knew he was
being heard,

"You know I want this traitor dead too. I'd stick him myself if we didn't
need him—but we do". Malik was still staring at him, but hadn't taken the
lethally filled needle out of Brother's vain completely. David watched him
carefully; he dared not excite nor upset him, so he spoke in a whisper, with
extraordinary composure, "Just give me that smack man, we'll save it for

later. We'll do this together—later. I promise. Don't press man. Just pull it out. You can do this Malik."

Malik's eyes were dancing crazily. The nerves in his face were twitching and he was breathing as if he was trying to catch his breath. But David had some kind of magic about him, like Justice, he had the power to command others with ease. The longer he looked Malik directly in the eyes, the more difficult Malik found it not to stare back at David. And the longer he stared, the easier it was for him to listen to the pair of lips moving before him seemingly at first, without sound, until he was able to calm down and tune in to David's station. David had begun to take deep, long, exaggerated inhalations as well. Slowly, Malik began to follow suit. David watched intently as Malik's eyebrows lifted little by little, while his shoulders moved lower than his neck. He turned and looked downward, then began to pull the needle out of Brother's newly reopened vein. Air unable to escape for the last ten minutes blasted gruffly from Brother's nostrils in half-second expulsions exhaled between open-mouthed elongated gasps. His last and next life had both flashed across his eyes in the past ten minutes. He knew Malik was milliseconds away from filling his favorite vain with enough of the white lady for three junkies to overdose. It came so close to actually happening, he was now soaked with his own urine. Brother had seen the vision of his own dead body reflected in Malik's dilated pupils and was so convinced he was about to meet Satan; he had extended his arm to shake the devil's hand. David grabbed the dangling hand and yanked Brother's entire body into an erect stance with one pull. That's when Malik began to beat Brother like a runaway slave—with his bare hands. He definitely broke a few ribs when he let off a twenty-punch drum roll into Brother's mid-section.

"Now we can go," he grunted towards David, barely out of breath.
"Malik, I need you to relax brother."
"I'm cool now, man. I'm all-right."

He looked Malik in the eye again as they pulled Brother up from the floor.

"I need you with me brother, we have work to do and brothers are scarce. Can you hang?"

"I got your back David. I'm on it."

"Let's get up to Big Hannah's. That's where Papa Joe is. Passion's bound to show sooner or later. And, you know Papa Joe has a plan."

"Cool. I'm down."

David grabbed Brother's left arm and threw it over his own shoulder. Malik just positioned the weight of his left, opened palm under Brother's right underarm and squeezed his upper-arm so tightly, it made Brother's chest protrude and his head lift. They headed down Stone Avenue and eased over to Dumont, where the light was dim. It was about 4:00 in the morning now, and most of the looting and rioting had ceased. Pigs were still crawling all over Browns' Village though. They were looking for Passion. They were looking for Papa Joe too. They knew he was the grandfather and was sure he would know where Passion was hiding. Anne had been at the precinct most of the night. She heard about what Passion had done at the hospital while she was inquiring about how to bring charges up against the police officer that had killed Deuce.

They had called Passion a crazed lunatic; and planned to take her to Kings County General's "G" Building for the mentally insane. Anne heard the transmission go over the dispatcher's special frequency, "She's approximately five feet, eight inches, one hundred thirty pounds, dark skinned, female black, torn and bloody blue sleeveless knit, armed with a knife, dangerously deranged Emotionally Disturbed Person E- D-P–APPROACH WITH CAUTION."

"What the hell happened at that hospital?" Anne mumbled to herself, trying not to show her concern too much. She also overheard the officers talking.

"If we find her, we do make sure we teach her a lesson they all will remember."

"That's right. New York City police officers stick together. We can't let civilians think they can get away with attacking us."

Anne couldn't help but to chime in at that point,

"Oh, I guess it doesn't matter that he killed her son. And I guess it doesn't matter that her father-in-law saved that same officer's life when the mob of angry Negroes were ready to lynch him? I suggest that you leave her to mourn and let him lick his wounds. He's the murderer here—and we will teach him a lesson he won't forget if he gets away with it."

The officers started moving closer to her, but Anne started shouting real loud, " I ain't afraid of you cracker cops—what you gonna do now—beat me up and kill my sons? Huh? What y'all wanna do?"

The newsman sitting in the corner was writing it all down. He got up to let Anne know he was on her side. The cops saw that Anne had an ally. Afraid of what he would publicize, they backed off.

"Don't worry Miss. You and your friend will be protected. My name is Sam Furman and I will write your story and have it printed in tomorrow's Daily, with your permission of course.

"Only if you promise to tell the truth about what's happened to my friend Passion. She's the one whose son was shot today. She's out there somewhere and they're hunting her down like a dog."

Sam appeared to be trustworthy, and Anne thought if he exposed the truth about Deuce's murder, it would take the heat off of Passion. She started to talk to Sam as if they were the best of friends. She told him almost everything she knew about Passion—about how she met Passion, and how the community felt about Passion and her family. She retold the tragic murder of Justice, Passion's brothers and her parents. She relived the birth of each child, and each trial Passion endured throughout her life including the clean get-a -way they all had made earlier, the day before in Whitestone. She talked more in ten minutes to that one person than she had ever spoken to any one in one sitting. And, she especially had never talked that much to any white man without feeling threatened, nervous or embarrassed. The possibility of saving Passion had given Anne courage. She knew this was something she must do.

Sam, on the other hand, was a novice at his profession. He was fresh out of Brooklyn College–a Journalism Major–and scared to death to be out in a "colored" neighborhood at this time of night. He was a mouse of a man whose voice could only be heard if it was read–and he remained anonymous. He even looked like a mouse. He wore black, horn-rimmed Clark Kent glasses, a short-sleeve white cotton shirt which hadn't stained with one bead of sweat all day, a side-parted wet look hair style, and an expression that cried, "Please don't hit me, I've been beat up everyday of my life". He had arrived at the precinct about 5 P.M. on a tip he had gotten from the sports editor who had told Sam about the riot in Browns' Village and suggested the precinct as a guaranteed and safe spot for a major scoop. From the time he had gotten there the cops had treated him like he was invisible. He hadn't the gumption to be very demanding, but he had refused to leave the station. When they would suggest that he find information on the street, he nervously repeated the first article of The Bill of Rights…" Congress shall make no law respecting an establishment of religion, or prohibiting the free exercise thereof; or abridging the freedom of speech or of the *PRESS*; or the right of the people peaceably to assemble and to petition the Government for a redress of grievances." After the fifth time they put him in the corner adjacent to the holding pen and treated him like he was invisible for the rest of the night.

"He wants to exercise his rights to interview looters, let him interview looters," one officer had said dryly. Then they'd laughed every time they looked at him back there.

"I'll fix them," Sam repeated all night as he sat and wrote his most prolific and passionate article in his career, "Cop Child-killer." He wondered if he should use all k's as he retaliated with his pen. That would do it. Then he heard Anne confronting the officers in the front. She was just the person he needed.

"I know it's late, but is there anywhere we can go to talk? He asked.

"It's 4 in the morning. There's only one place I can think of, and I pray I'm doing the right thing. Let's go to Big Hip Hannah's; there's more than just food to please you."

"I beg your pardon."

"Don't worry. It's safe and Hannah is the best cook in Browns' Village. Are you driving?" She was whispering now and gesturing him to stop speaking as two officers looked suspiciously at them while they passed. She walked out of the door, not feeling comfortable talking right there inside of the precinct.

"I'm parked over here."

She walked in the direction he was pointing and confessed, "I'm glad you're driving, some hot heads may still be out and they're more than ready to kill a white boy tonight. But if you just take this next left on to Rockaway Avenue, we'll be on our way to get you the story of your life. And, we'll make sure you get out of Browns' Village alive."

Sam was trying not to look so scared. He was hoping Anne wasn't paying attention to his shaking hands moving so violently they were making the steering wheel shake as well. But the shaking stopped immediately when Sam and Anne both gasped simultaneously, astounded at the vision before them. They had approached Pitkin Avenue at the light. Sam accurately described it as, "Modern day ruins—my God. This place looks like

Old Rome or Greece. These people must have been more than outraged to ravage their own home this way."

"That's what people like you don't realize. This could never be our home. White America will never allow it. Whenever Black people become independent or affluent they either kill them, rob them or buy them off. And whenever a so-called officer of the law has the right to just shoot our children down in the street, you better believe the Old South is alive and well right here in the North. Damn just look at this." Anne was more disgusted and angry than she realized. Everything Passion had ever told her was very clear at this time. For once she finally understood that America was not the land of opportunity for her people—not unless you wanted an opportunity to be a slave again. She finally felt the anger and the pain Passion and Justice had always expressed.

Pitkin Avenue was unrecognizable. As Browns' Village's central shopping area it would be sorely missed. Sam slowed down almost to a complete halt. A cool breeze was sweeping through the street circumvolving the light weight debris in small tornadoes—picking up, then dropping anything from paper bags to broken 45 lp's or children's clothing hoisted earlier by a careless looter. Every store had been burned, some worse than others, but they all had been looted. Each building looked as if it had been condemned for over 10 years. What damage the looters hadn't done, the Fire Department did when it came through. The merchandise that hadn't been stolen was destroyed. Toys and stationery from Woolworth's rolled or blew down the street, shoes from Bakers and Tom McCann lay amongst sheets and towels from the linen store. The pizzeria's front window was shattered and the inside was covered in soot and damage machinery. Expensive sneakers and sporting gear from Pro's Sport Shop was lying about as well. Anne was trying to take in as much as she could as Sam picked up speed and asked for directions again. He began to drive as fast as he could, stunned by his surroundings. His eyes were oscillating like those of a cat clock—wide and mechanical. He was looking for deranged looters, expecting them to dash out at him. But they had all gone home or to jail for the night.

Anne instructed Sam to drive under the el and take a left right into the dark alleyway, which was the rear of Hannah's place. The street was lightless and it frightened Sam. Anne peeped the shaking steering wheel.

"Don't worry Sam I am. Everyone here is definitely friend–not foe." Then she laughed, "A foe wouldn't have the heart."

Sam's headlights lit up Big Hannah's "No Trespassers" red and white sign; his heart leapt when the dogs viciously barked at his unfamiliar scent. But Anne, surprised at her own nerve, jumped out of the car and beckoned the dogs to her. She was so anxious to get Sam inside, she forgot to be scared. Anne nodded to Hannah and Papa Joe, armed with his Saturday night special and standing at the door; then she motioned to Sam to come out.

"I'm a friend," he assured Papa Joe and stepped out of the car with both hands in the air. "I'm a reporter sir, a reporter for the Daily. I want to write about what really happened here and I'm going to tell the truth."

"Show him in. We have a big surprise for both of you."

Anne fenced the dogs off and flashed a big grin at Sam. "See, I told you. Come on."

He followed her inside the red door that was usually being held open so that a drunk could be tossed out of it. Sam was amazed to see the expensive decor within Big Hip Hannah's private palace. It was all so unexpected. From the outside one wouldn't expect to see plush velvet high Victorian chairs and soft black leather couches, ceiling fans, chandeliers, mahogany tables, paneled walls and some of the most expensive crystal and china in Brooklyn. Sam could imagine her home filled with happy people milling about, dancing, and singing, as they would stand around the baby grand piano he noticed parked in the grandiose, red room.

"Who *is* this woman?" he whispered to Anne. Anne simply shook her indicating to him not to speak.

Papa Joe, who walked behind Hannah directed Anne and Sam towards the blue room—a very cozy room used for watching television and fire side chats, and led them to the bright, silvery kitchen where Passion sat at the huge white tiled and pine country kitchen table. A steaming cup of hot coffee was in front of her and Tres was in her lap. He was gripping her waist and sobbing silently upon her breast, and she was caressing him like he was a newborn baby. But her presence didn't surprise them as much as her unexpected composure. She was breathing controllably. She sat erect and alert. She didn't even appear to be tired and it was 5 o'clock in the morning.

"Does she look like an emotionally disturbed person Sam?" Anne challenged him. "Make sure you write about her appearance and emotional state and imagine what those cops would've done to her if they had gotten their hands on her." She ran to Passion, dropped to her knees and joined Tres in a suffocating love grip. Passion began to weep as well. "I'm so glad you're all right Passion. I'm so glad to have you back safe."

"The pigs are still crawling all over your building though, so you gotta stay put", David spoke as he walked into the room. "What's up with the white boy?"

Papa Joe explained, "He's a reporter," Sam was trying to smile. David's militant clothing reminded him of the California Black Panther Party he had heard so much about. He's going to write about our side of the story and let the world know just what is going on here in Browns' Village. Once the news is exposed, Whitey is gonna have to back off. They been killing our family members since before we were put on the boat and I'm tired of it.

Hannah pulled a chair out for Papa Joe to sit in and motioned to everyone to have a seat at the extremely large table. Miss Lucy got two pots of coffee and sat them on the table after she distributed cups and saucers with the efficiency of a high quality waitress. Papa Joe sat at the head of one end and Mama Lettie, who had gotten there earlier, sat at the other end. David and Anne sat on either side on Passion. And Sam sat across from Passion and right next to Big Hip Hannah. The story they told him took three pots of coffee, a light breakfast and two hours. He knew it wouldn't make the early edition, but the four star, late edition would have an extra that would shock the world–"Decades of Death–The Price of Freedom for Africans in America", was what he would end up calling it. Passion started:

"Well Mr. Furman, the first thing you need to know is that, the murder of my son yesterday is just one of the attacks against my family in over the last six years. They killed my parents in 1957, my brothers in 1958 and then my husband in 1961."

"Who is *they* Mrs. Freeman?"

Papa Joe answered, "The national Klansmen–that's who. They've been after us for years–us and every other black person who escaped southern Mississippi. You don't know nothing about *that* young man; not unless you're from down there. And you don't look or sound like you're from down there. You couldn't bear it if you had to live there–it's a different world." Papa Joe went on to explain how he and Reverend Franklin had switched identities to throw the Gourmand family off, but how they always caught up with them. He explained how Gourmand was a big name in shipping and how they manipulated the unions, railroads, and politicians off of the backs of African slaves in Mississippi.

"You mean to tell me there are still slaves in the south?" Sam was aghast and appalled. And now afraid to write what Papa Joe was telling him. "Well how are these people connected to the police force in New York City? Are you telling me they can pull strings all the way up here?

"I'm telling you", Papa Joe said dryly. He looked deeply into Sam's eyes and saw fear beginning to consume him. Passion was frowning at Sam. And when she looked around the table, each face she gazed into had the same look of disgust and disappointment.

"Come on now Sam I am—you wanted a great story and I delivered. Now it's time to eat the green eggs and ham." Anne was jokingly serious, "Don't chicken out now."

David was squinting. He had kept his head throughout most of the ordeal and he felt his composure slipping out of his grasp. He wasn't sure if he liked the idea of trusting this white boy and he was afraid Sam would hear Brother, who was tied up in the back, in Fat Back's old room. Malik was standing guard.

"What's the problem Sam?"

"Oh, oh no problem, no problem. I'm just trying to decide the best angle to take. I mean we're dealing with dirty cops here. Nobody likes dirty cops. But we need concrete proof. I can't expose these Gourmand people without months of investigation at the very least. When this story hits the stands, I would love for this cop to go down for sure. I want him just like I want that Aryan bastard Herzog that lives in Whitestone. He's been recruiting for the Klan for years and no one can get a jail sentence to stick on him. He knows too many people.

"Herzog!!!" everyone screamed in unison almost awaking Tres who had fallen asleep on the couch.

"I was rolling in the dirt with that son-of-a-bitch yesterday", Passion shared, "What do you know about him?"

"I know he's connected. They've had him on everything from murder to kidnapping—and he always gets off. And his victims are always Negro boys. He also smuggles drugs on the "G" Express. The railroad that runs on the southeast lines. It's got to pass right through here. Aryans have been making a mint trafficking narcotics throughout poor, small towns and big cities this side of the country. I've been following them for a while, but my chief editor won't give the okay on the exclusive."

"Man, don't you see we're talking about the same people?"

Papa Joe could have gone through the floor, instead he had jumped to his feet. "G is for Gourmand. The former slave traders and plantation owners—our enemy!" he thought to himself.

Everyone was quiet for moment. They were all shocked at the uncanny coincidence. And then they went to work. Each person simultaneously pulled his or her chair closer to the other and they commenced to outline the story that would rock the country. Eight people had died and fifty-nine had been jailed. Millions in damages had been assessed and the police officer that caused it all lay in a hospital bed being waited on hand and foot as if he was the victim. Sam, carrying his thin, leather strapped brief-case and new courage left to accomplish his mission at 7 a.m. And as soon as they were sure that he was gone, they dragged Brother out of the back and initiated part 2 of the plan.

"Just kill me, just kill me. I'm better off dead. Give me the shot, man. Come on David, just give me the shot."

"Shut the hell up Brother, or I will give you a shot—right in your mouth. Better yet, I'll let Malik whip your sorry ass for you. So just shut up. You're gonna work for your freedom boy."

Papa Joe was standing over Brother, trying not to hit him—trying not to hate him. Trembling with anger. Looking at Brother encouraged Papa Joe's spirit to want to purge itself of every ounce of hatred for racism and the Klan, their lynching and other evil deeds, but mostly, his hatred for Gourmand—any Gourmand that existed. He thought he wanted to hit him, finally hit him with all of his strength and pain. But then he looked into Brother's eyes and saw nothing. There was no joy, no love—no life. And for the first time, he really saw just Brother. Papa Joe suddenly wondered how a child became this lost. For the first time, he felt Brother who was limp and practically weightless. Then finally, for the first time, he listened to what Brother was really saying; he hadn't wanted to accept the inevitable conclusion Brother consistently prophesied speaking incessantly, as he begged and whined. They tried everything they could think of to shut him up, but two hours had passed and Brother was still saying the same damn thing—over and over and over again,

"Just kill me. Come on David, just give me the shot. Come on David, come on man—just kill me."

David was ready to slap him silly, but Papa Joe grabbed his open-faced hand right before it landed across Brother's cheek.

"We want him to look good, David. Maintain your cool—brother. You've been an essential part of saving my family and there's nothing I wouldn't do for you. I love you for laying your life down for us—but I need to know if you're willing to play this all the way out."

"Well what do you want him to do? He's like a dying horse Pops, I can't take *his* pain anymore."

"Well he's going to help us get rid of our problem at the hospital. As soon as Murphy's out of the way, the pigs will ease up off of Passion. So we need to get him up and looking good 'cause we're going to the hospital."

"Sounds good to me."

Passion had gone into the blue room to talk to Mama Lettie and re-entered upon hearing the word hospital.

"What's happening Papa? What are we gonna do?"

"You don't have to worry about a thing, baby. Papa's gonna make sure that when you wake up, you will have no other concerns outside of saying good-bye to Deuce—you've been through enough."

"I already did that Papa. But go ahead and do your thing–I know you got to. I'm a talk to Mama Lettie a bit, then I'm going to sleep over there next to Tres." Looking at him as she spoke, she could see a look she never saw on Papa Joe before. He was looking at her so intently; she felt his love and sincere concern. "I'm all right Papa Joe. I'm all right. I'll tell you all about it later. I'll never be the same. I'll tell you that.

"I know it was rough girl. I know. But you made it through!"

"Yes I did!" She grabbed him around his neck and just lingered there for a moment. "I'll see you later."

"All right Passion. I'll be back real soon. This won't take long."

She watched the three men and Brother walk out of the door and drive off in Papa Joe's dodge. And Passion knew their mission was a lethal one–someone was bound to die. She wondered if they were finally gonna off Brother. She couldn't agree with killing any brother–especially Brother–without trying to re-program him. Then again, it's next to impossible to change anyone who loves hating himself–as Mama Lettie always said. And Brother was in lust with his pain.

They had cleaned him up pretty well. He was wearing one of Papa Joe's dashikis, David's shoes and black beret. No one would ever recognize him dressed this way. Every once in a while, as they rode along, Malik would slap him in the back of his head.

"You better not 'f' this up Brother. I will beat you to death. You hear me boy. You'll beg me to shoot you for all the pain I will make you feel."

"I'm already in pain Malik. You gotta give me a little hit. Just to make sure I get it right. I'll walk straighter if you give me some of that white leg. Come on Malik. I know you still got it."

"Negro please. I'll hook you up all right. As soon as you get the job done."

"For real man?!"

"Yeah, I'm for real."

David was looking at Malik in the rear view mirror like he was crazy. Malik shook his head real quick to indicate that he wasn't serious.

David and Papa Joe exchanged glances. They knew they were going to have to deal with Malik as soon as this was over. It was clear that he needed some healing too. But right now, he was the perfect brother to handle Brother.

They parked on Rochester Avenue, around the corner from Unity Hospital. Before they got out of the car, Malik had Brother cook up the foil packet and fill the needle.

"Remember," Malik taunted with Brother, "you get none of this if you screw this up. Do you know what to say?"

Brother nodded his head. His eyes and thoughts were on the needle and how he wished it were for him.

"I know what to say. I won't screw it up Malik. I told you, I been working with this clown for a long time. He been getting information through me for years. I know he answers to that big pig uptown. All of the crooked pigs do. Believe me man, when I make him believe that big pig O'Connor sent word to him, he'll break." He looked at Malik pleadingly, "A little hit?"

"Don't forget. I'm right outside that room. Papa Joe is in the staircase. David is in the elevator. Brothers are all over this hospital and up and down this street. We'll get you away from the hospital quickly. But if you try to escape, you're gonna wish you were that pig."

Brother stuck out his chest and stood as straight as he possibly could. He slipped the lethal dose of heroin up the bottom of his sleeve and held it there with his middle finger. He followed David, who led them all into the side door labeled Emergency Room in bright red letters. They all entered one-by-one and sat in the Emergency Room. As soon as one of the nurses on duty went inside, David went to the desk to distract the lone worker. Malik and Brother slid into the nearby staircase and ran quietly up to the second floor and down the hall where Passion told them the pig was stashed. Room 232.

It was a camouflaged closet—set off from the other rooms on the floor. There was a uniform sitting in the room with him, and another one outside the room. The officer posted inside of room 232 was fast asleep. And the one outside was just waking up. They watched him as he squirmed and stretched. He looked in the room and then down each hall—then he went to the bathroom down the hall.

Malik and Brother dashed into the room. Malik quickly slipped his arms up under the sleeping officer's shoulders, and put him in a sleeper hold he learned in wrestling. In a swift twist the pig was unconscious. And, Brother beheld his tormentor. No one—not even Fat Back knew of the torture this man had put him through. Brother was more than happy to make this pig disappear. Unfortunately, Brother had always been so afraid of him, he wasn't sure his nerve would hold up. But then he thought of Fat Back, and how he turned Fat Back against him, taking away the only friend he ever had.

He first met Officer Murphy in the train yards when he and Fat Back had gone for a pick up. They didn't even know Murphy was a cop at first because he was always dressed in street clothes when he came to the yards. Nobody liked him either. Not even the other white guy. Murphy always made ignorant remarks, or racist remarks or would try to quote some cliché and get it all wrong. Brother was real nervous around him, mostly because of the way Murphy looked at Brother. He'd stare Brother down with his beady eyes. And he always grinned slyly at him like he knew something private about Brother. Brother would just put the most disgusted face he could contort, and then roll his eyes at him. Murphy loved making the insecure and neglected colored boy uncomfortable and made it a ritual.

He snuck up on Brother one day in the street when he was wearing his blues. Then he chased him knowing Brother was scared to death of being stopped by the cops and probably wouldn't recognize him. He laughed as he shoved Brother into an alley separating two stores on Sutter Avenue. He snatched his own hat off and cracked up laughing.

"It's me boy! It's me–Officer Murphy!! Ha–Haaa. Boy you should've seen the look on your face when you thought the cops were after ya!"

Brother was out of breath but tried to smile back; almost relieved to know it was Murphy,

"Yeah, that was real funny Officer Murphy. Look I gotta go." He tried to walk passed Murphy who was at least a foot taller than Brother and kept grabbing him by the back of his collar.

"Don't be afraid of me boy. I'm your friend. Look, I got something for you."

Murphy pulled out a thick, foil packet filled with heroin. Brother tried to run again, afraid of whatever this pig had in mind. He was holding the packet between his thumb and forefinger and dangled it in front of Brother like bait.

"I just want to share with you some of what we get off the trains. I mean what you're pushing around here with Fat Back has been cut, sliced and diced. This here is pure heroin. And after you taste this–you're gonna be my customer. As a matter of fact, you're gonna be my slave."

He dragged Brother, kicking and screaming, into the side door to the tenement apartment building on the other end of the alley. They ducked under a fire escape ladder and Murphy pulled the stunned Brother through a cellar window. Brother shrunk in fear. He had no defense.

"I don't, I don't,–I don't wanna be no junkie. Please–I never took no smack man," Brother stuttered in a whisper.

"Come on Brother. Life has been rough, you deserve to take a vacation."

Murphy slapped Brother around, and then threw him like a rag doll all over the dirty basement floor. He cooked up the smack while Brother lay semi-conscious on a discarded mattress. He placed one knee in Brother's groin, and the other in his skinny chest, pinning his arms to the floor under Brother's back.

"Remember that I control you boy. I'm your god. I'll feed you when you need to be fed, just as long as you do what I say." He stuck the needle directly in Brother's vein, better than a well-trained triage nurse. He dropped the half-filled needle there beside Brother and climbed through the cellar window to resume his beat.

Brother thought of all the pain he had caused others once he got strung out. The lives he stole, and the soul he sold. He looked at Murphy's gauze covered face.

"Hey Murphy, guess what—it's your turn. I think you need a vacation."

Murphy recognized Brother's voice right away, "Brother the Junkie! My old slave. Won't you do ole massa' a favor and bring me that cup with a straw. I need a drink. What's this about a vacation?"

"Everybody knows the truth Murphy", Brother was right in the pig's ear, he whispered in venom, his voice shaking the whole time, "I just finished talking to a newspaper man. I told him everything. I even mentioned O' Conner. I told them how you been getting fat off all of the dirty work O' Conner sends down for you. How you had me kill the Franklins and set up Fat Back. I confessed enough to send me to jail, and you to Hell. Cops ain't even looking for Passion no more; they're all talking about what a disgrace to the department you are and whether you gonna get your retirement money or not."

"How'd you get in my room boy?" Murphy attempted to scream, but Brother covered his mouth. Malik was watching from behind the door.

He kicked the unconscious pig in the head whenever he thought the pig had moved.

Brother was talking a little louder now, "What do you think happened to your protection? They all left, *man*. It's all over. So why don't you leave now too?"

Brother took the needle out. The same needle Malik had filled for his demise. The same needle he had begged for earlier. He tied the plastic cord around the pig's arm and placed the needle in his trembling white hands.

"Don't worry Murphy. You'll have plenty of company in Hell. I'll probably meet you there myself real soon."

Brother walked out, forcefully closing the door as quietly as he could. Malik tip-toed out before him and was waiting near the staircase. He saw the second pig coming and motioned to Brother to hurry up.

Murphy immediately felt Brother's absence. The wind that blew in as Brother closed the door was to be the last fresh air Murphy would ever feel. He pushed his behind back and propped himself up on his pillow as much as he possibly could. And, he stared down through the gauze at the tiny, thin, deadly, silver object he held. The possibility of relief through finality urged his hand to point the needle towards his arm. Visions of the wives he had beaten and lost. The children he had abandoned. The people he had turned on to smack and blackmailed into every criminal activity Browns' Village now possessed. He thought of Deuce, and the headlines of the Daily—"Krooked Kop Kills Kids."

He stuck it in. He pressed the syringe gradually, until every drop of the drug was now inside of him. Euphoria set in. Murphy dazzlingly watched the white lady gallop up his arm and into his head. He closed his eyes and welcomed her with opened arms. His entire body began to shake violently; his bed thumped against the floor, bouncing so hard it caused the glass on the dresser to fall and break. As the glass shattered, Murphy died. The unconscious cop outside the door was startled out of his sleep. Nurses ran in from the nurses' station to find him stretching forth, eyes bulging and a needle still stuck in his vein. They ripped open his gown and attempted to revive his heart, but to no avail. Papa Joe drove like a bat out of Hell. Brother sat like a stone in the back of the car. He was reborn; and his conscious returned.

When he arrived at Big Hannah's there was solemness in the air. Miss Lucy, Big Hannah, Passion and Tres were all sitting around the television watching the consequences of the night before. The aftermath had been more horrific than they'd ever imagined. Folks uptown in Harlem were still looting. They were running from the police and water-hose armed firemen who were spraying them down like dogs. The weight of the thrusting velocity ripped clothes off bodies, hair out of heads and slapped the picketers and looters against the brick walls. They fell to the ground yelling, "NO JUSTICE, NO PEACE–NO JUSTICE, NO PEACE!" Passion reared back and cringed at the irony of it all.

"Amen," she added.

She looked up at Papa Joe, "What are you thinking Papa? I know that look -what's on your mind?"

"It's time for me to put an end to this madness for once and for all. Your daddy told me about how he left Mississippi 30 years ago. And those crackers down there are still trying to kill him. There has to be a connection between the heroin, the Gourmand's and the trains that run through here. Justice was always telling me about how he would spy on the white men down at the train yards and the cargo he saw them trading and selling illegally. Some of that cargo was heroin. Ain't that right Brother?"

"That's absolutely right Papa Joe. I can give you a couple of names. Better still, I can show y'all where their stash is kept. I'll take y'all. I want to go."

"So we can trust you now Brother? "

"You can trust me Papa Joe," Brother was looking at the floor, "but I can understand why anyone wouldn't want to. I don't deserve anybody's trust, love or concern. I helped destroy your lives and I know that. And today–today you helped me get rid of the demon that who has put me through hell for the last five years. I could never thank you enough for that. I'll do anything for anybody here- any time you want. And once I get clean again…I'm a stay clean and straight."

They were all just standing there looking at Brother. No one really knew how to react. They wanted to forgive him, respect him and love him, but they all couldn't just yet. Passion walked out of the room. Mama Lettie and Lucy followed her. Malik wanted to say something, but couldn't quite get it out. So he just stood in front of Brother–shaking his head, holding his lips tightly closed. Big Hip Hannah and Papa Joe took turns embracing him, then holding him as he broke down and cried. Then David, with tears in his eyes and flash backs of the third grade dashing across his memory, walked over and stood Brother up,

"Paul. Brother Paul, I can love you, but only if you can love you. You got to see that you're a victim too. The white man simply used you as an overseer for us–city field niggers. You need to love you and hate who hurt you and how they made you hurt your own."

"I do brother. I do."

There was a long pause. Then the sound of a glass shattering in the kitchen jolted everyone.

"Let's get to work," Papa Joe was but for so much sentiment right now, "I want y'all to go down to the train yards and see what Brother can help y'all find. If you can get a name that will connect the Mississippi Gourmand's to the Klan up here, I'll have all I need. I'm pretty sure I know who is responsible for the drug traffic and how it's being sent, but I need more information before we can bring them down. Once you get me those necessary names, then I need to see a man about a dog."

Passion had come back in the room holding up the broken glass so no one would be alarmed. She overheard Papa Joe speaking.

"I don't know Papa Joe. I don't know about this. I need you alive. Tres and the girls need you too. Please don't go. Why don't you just send the brothers? They can go."

Mama Lettie grabbed his arm and escorted him into the next room, waving behind her back to everyone else to leave the talking to her. David led Malik and Brother out of the front door. And the two elders sat in the blue room facing one another. They both let out deep sighs and moans. Lettie held his hand.

"I know what you're thinking Joseph Franklin," she smiled as she spoke to him in a voice that took him back forty years or more, " I know that no one realizes that you and Justice switched identities, but I don't think those white folk even care anymore. Justice Freeman is on an old hit list of theirs. This thing is bigger than all of us now. It's like since crackers couldn't control us anymore they had to find a new way to destroy us all."

"That's exactly why I gotta go."

"What are you gonna do?" she asked painfully, knowing what he was thinking, "what are you gonna do?"

"I'm going to do what the reverend would've done. I'm gonna do what I know I gotta do. I'm gonna save the rest of my family. I'm gonna make sure, not another one is snatched away–just feet from me."

Papa Joe was trembling now. It was all finally starting to hit him. His lips quivered, so he stopped trying to speak. Lettie tried to hold his hand, but he violently shook it a loose.

"I'm tired Lettie. I'm tired and I gotta go."

The 56-year-old elder jumped up, then stood with a force one wouldn't dare reckon with. He looked down at his old friend and glared at her, staring deeply into her eyes and she knew there was no more she could say to him. Lettie dropped her head in prayer, unable to watch as he quietly walked out of the back door.

Miss Lucy was still sitting in front of the television–shocked at the devastating effect of the night before on the black neighborhoods throughout the city being shown. Suddenly she screeched at the top of her lungs. Everybody came running from the kitchen.

"Listen, listen, listen!" She was hopping in her seat and pointing at the black and white screen. She had just heard the newscaster say that they wanted to speak to the mother of the murdered boy and it was rumored that Reverend Martin Luther King was coming to support her. Then they all started yelling and screaming.

"See Papa Joe!" Passion was yelling, "here comes our help right now!" But it was too late. Martin King meant nothing to Papa Joe anymore. "Where's Papa Joe Mama Lettie–where did he go?"

"I'm sorry child," she was mumbling and holding back her tears, "you can't stop any man from doing what he's got to do, Papa Joe is gone. Let's just pray he'll make it back safely."

The novelty of Dr. King wore off real fast. Hannah and Lucy joined the two and they all prayed.

"RETROSPECTION"

Back to the wood
Back to the 'hood
Back to the people that ain't no damn good

Back to the fight
the stolen birthright
is about to be taken back into the night
no one in sight–taken in flight
'til the time for taking *everything* back is right

Sankofa–go back
get the life you once had
daily rituals, the spirit,
the good and the bad
find brothers and sisters,
your father, your mother
read the rules that demand we look out for each other

Get *every*thing back
royalty redeems
in more than
fried chicken and healing dreams,
macaroni and cheese, and shady trees
we've got all these,
but the ancestors then,
we'll surely please
when they gaze upon us standing righteously
affirming the future, focused and free

Sankofa–go back
get the life you once had
daily rituals, the spirit
the good and the bad,
find brothers and sisters
your father, your mother
read the rules that demand we look out for each other.

C. Wright-Lewis 8/9/99

CHAPTER NINE

"RETROSPECTION"

Mississippi, The Delta
July 18, 1963

His '63 Chevy moved at top speed, as if the airport would close down if he didn't get there right away, as if Mississippi would run if it heard he was coming, as if he would die if he delayed his action one solitary minute more. Papa Joe was possessed with the new revelation of his life's objective and could now see what he needed to do. He was sick and tired of the white man playing God with his family, snatching their lives at will, breaking his children's hearts and now trying to destroy his village and every African village in America, contaminating each one with heroin—the new slave chain. Joseph Justice Freeman a.k.a. Joseph Franklin knew it was his fate to confront the devil head on. And he couldn't wait.

He used his private stash of cash for his flight to Jackson, Mississippi—the stash he planned to buy school clothes with and surprise Passion and the children. But everything had changed. Insuring their lives was his main priority now—by any means necessary.

In a record twenty minutes, he arrived at the New York International Airport in Queens that was soon to be named after the soon to be assassinated President Kennedy. He picked up a flight on Eastern Airlines that would have him in the delta by 3:30. The new Boeing 727 jet that Papa Joe swore he would never set foot on didn't make him the least bit nervous. Looking at its famed silver t-tail glimmering in the bright sunlight as he walked towards the mobile staircase, made the young elder feel like he was mounting a giant ibis sent by the gods to fly him to his divinely-appointed destination. It was nothing like the jets used in the world war. The magical, shiny machinery fascinated him for a moment, but he was too angry to focus on the airplane for but so long. His adrenaline was pumping through his body at an unhealthy rate. Secretly, he knew that he was really too upset to act on any decisions he was making right now, and he thought for a second that perhaps he should not go. But he knew he couldn't live with himself if he didn't. He had to go. This had gone too far and he was just too through.

Joe also knew that once the brothers found out that he had left, they would come down too. They knew he wanted Gourmand and knew he was planning to go one day. They just didn't know, today was the day. But they always had his back, and that made him feel sufficiently armed. He knew they were probably realizing right then what he and Sam had already confirmed. Gourmands owned the east coast train line. Hell, Gourmands owned most of Mississippi. But Gourmand didn't own him. He didn't even know Papa Joe. He had known the reverend before he escaped and probably had a hit out on him and his whole family. That's why practically the whole family had been killed—including Justice.

"But the sons of bitches don't know me," he told himself as the plane ascended into the cloudless, blue sky.

He motioned to the stewardess to ask for a drink. He noticed her watching him from afar with a look of concern on her face. He wanted her to know he was all right; he had his fill with drama for a lifetime. He knew he had to calm down—the flight was about three hours long, so he knew he needed to smolder his fire. He hadn't any sleep in the last 24 hours, and after all of the drama, he looked as haggard as he felt. He decided he needed a nap.

"Let me have a scotch sweetheart—make it a double."

The neatly tucked, shorthaired flight attendant seemed relieved that he was preparing to relax. She had just attended a workshop that taught her to identify disturbed passengers and up 'til now, Papa Joe fit the build.

"Have a nice nap sir," she added to the smile she gave as she handed him the drink.
"Thank-you, but please wake me in two hours. I don't want to sleep too long."
"My pleasure."

Papa Joe was asleep before he could finish the drink. But his nightmare would not allow him to sleep the full two hours. He couldn't erase Deuce's bloody face from his restless mind. His victimized grandson kept calling to him.
"Papa Joe, Papa Joe...please help me Papa Joe..."
"I'm coming!!" Papa Joe yelled aloud, startling all of the passengers.
"Sorry," he mumbled, looking in the direction of Suzie—his stewardess.

She smiled, but squinted her eyes in suspicion.

Papa Joe sat up straight and watched the green landscapes below. It amazed him how the earth looked as if God had sketched it out on canvas, then painted it with brilliant colors from the rainbow. And since it was a clear day, he could see the world without a cloud destroying his view. If he was able, he would've enjoyed it, but nothing could give him pleasure now. He was on a mission he didn't he could survive.

Passion and the children crossed his mind—Justice too. He grinned at the thought of his only son, and then once again vowed to avenge his seed.

He spotted the East Line Express and saluted downward. Short stacks of white smoke were sent in return. Papa Joe knew the diesel could take him to the divinely appointed rendezvous point where he and Gourmand were destined to meet—to end the curse. Deceivingly appearing dazed, as he stared out of the plane's emergency window, the heroic grandfather plotted his course. Instructions popped in his mind in chronological order, from where to find his awaiting boxcar to how to get into Gourmand's warehouse. Feeling a metamorphosis-taking place, Papa Joe prepared his person for the unknown course he had begun. The purpose of his existence on the planet was before him. Apprehensive, yet receptive, he dove in.

As his foot touched Jackson, he gasped at the beauty of Mississippi. He recalled all of the stories the reverend had told him about the place he had called "Nature's Bounty." Magnanimous and wise weeping willows swept by the wind, nurtured by golden light floating in the aqua-colored ozone. Here rich soil had made royalty of cane, and cotton king. Magnolia blossoms reminded the visitor that God lived and loved the luxurious South as they freely floated in the breeze. Breath-takingly, the sight overwhelmed him, though Papa Joe also smelled the stench of slavery that still lingered in the air.

Mississippi's history of hanging and skinning Blacks was as popular as picking cotton, and Papa Joe revisited every memory passed on to him from his dear friend Reverend Franklin. From the time he stepped off of the plane, Papa Joe could hear "Rev" talking in his ear, describing the beauty of Mississippi, and the repeated warning of the evil that lurked there as well. Knowing what he knew and being from New York was bound to make him stand- out in attitude alone, let alone how he was dressed. He needed to change his clothes.

His first stop was at the second-hand clothing store. His new overalls and straw hat made him look like every other black man over 35, that's about when the strain of racism usually began to battle melanin's natural course and cause a man who would normally look 40 years old at sixty, look sixty years old at forty. He pulled the big brimmed straw hat over his forehead to avoid eye contact with anyone and headed for the freight yard. An elder of about eighty years was sitting on the porch outside of the store. He realized right away that Papa Joe was an unknown; he watched the younger elder walk down the road and silently prayed for his safety. He knew he'd be found out soon. The mocha chocolate, sunburnt elder had seen many come, but very few leave, had spent his entire life in slavery, and was now considered too old to be of any use. So they sat him on any porch he pleased and supplied him with wood from which he whittled animals and spiritual images. The whites had no idea that amongst the Negroes, he was actually a highly revered griot of the secret African society that lived within this modern ante-bellum south.

His name was After, he had been called that since he was a boy because no matter what event had occurred and how much anyone searched for him, he never showed up until after it was over. Crackers cracked their whips across his back time and time again, but it never changed his ways; they knew that about ten minutes after anything was over, After would show. He explained to spirit folks that his dead grandmother always warned him when a fire or something else was about to happen, and advised him to hide. She always spoke to him, and she was whispering to him right now.

It was After's life-long task to pass on the history of his people as told to him by his grandmother, a half African and half Cree whose parents had fled Florida and come to Mississippi together escaping Gourmand. Her mother had been Maurya. His rich, dark skin appeared to contrast his straight, jet-black hair; his deep brown dove-like eyes and his melodic, baritone voice made him easy to trust, and his cool, deliberate manner made him a perfect undercover leader. He slowly lifted the front of the extremely wide black brim of his old hat with the tip of his crooked middle finger, took a mental picture of Joe's frame and envisioned the path he had begun, and then dropped his head again.

In a trance, After watched the "city-fied" Papa Joe awkwardly trudge through the wild grass toward the train yard. It was about two o'clock in the afternoon, and the sun was just melting anything that tried to have breath. Anyone who lived in Mississippi knew better than to be outside this time of day, but Papa Joe was from New York, and he couldn't figure out why no one was around in the middle of the day. For a minute he thought he was in one of those "Twilight Zone" episodes and had taken a plane right into Hell. That's how hot it was.

He took off the tee shirt he had kept on for decency, and rolled the overalls past his stomach the second he climbed into the empty boxcar. His sweat dripped into his eyes quicker than he could wipe it away, so he wrapped the tee shirt around his head and pushed himself back into the corner behind the opened door. He was asleep before his head could hit the burlap sacks he found to be less irritating than he expected.

It was so quiet Papa Joe was startled out of his sleep by his own deep breathing. The unfamiliar surroundings confused him for a moment. He had drifted so deeply, murder and fire and hatred had left him free to dream. He began to grin, remembering what had happened last.

"Franklin," he said aloud, showed some teeth and shook his head. "That figures. Now what did he say?" He closed his eyes and attempted to revisit the conversations in the dream. There had been several brief encounters with his old friend Reverend Joseph Franklin; each time the reverend was a different age and in a different place, but each time he had said the same thing. "Listen to the lady, that's it! Listen to the lady."

He had been working so diligently trying to remember the dream; Papa Joe hadn't realized the train had begun to move. His head careened against the metal wall before he could move. Like a weightless scarecrow, his body was thrown back and forth as he tried to stand and jump out of the door. But it was "an exercise in futility," he thought to himself thinking of how "Rev" would've described the situation.

"Don't jump," he could've sworn he heard a woman's voice whispering as he looked around, " sshh...just listen".

He exhaled and loosened his shoulders enough for them to drop. Then he sat back on his behind, straightening and stretching his legs outward, out of the squatting position he had maneuvered. Papa Joe gripped the handle of the opened sliding boxcar door with his right hand, and slid down to allow his back to rest on the length of the metal door and raised his left knee to meet his hairy chest. His right foot settled in a safety niche behind a huge bolt on the step below the outside of the door. His left hand held his face in the direction of the wind, bracing it there with his anchored elbow. It was still hot, but the breeze from the moving train gave a false sense of cool as it beat the beads of sweat at the edge of his hairline back, causing them to gather and slide down his ears and into his graying sideburns.

He welcomed the waves of wind rapidly hitting his face, though the gentle slaps were soon to be a memory as he became transfixed by the passing trees. At first, they sat back about a half of a mile away, but about every two minutes, the distance decreased. By the time another five minutes had elapsed, they were a mere twenty feet away and Papa Joe began to think his squinting eyes were playing tricks on him. He thought he could see someone hiding behind a tree–darting out–then dashing behind another. It all happened in a matter of seconds since the train was moving so fast.

But after three flashes of color, he realized that there were people–black people–darting in and out of sight. Who were they hiding from? He wondered for a second, but all along, he knew.

"Damn–I done stepped into the past. I knew it was bad down here, but runaway slaves? God damn."

He was speaking aloud to himself and contemplating jumping off of the moving train. He definitely didn't wish to go in the direction they were fleeing. He suspected that he wasn't far from the Gulf; he could smell the water and noticed how the land was changing–becoming marsh-like. Then he began to see more and more escapees, their faces tight with fear and determination. His eyes locked with a young woman who reminded him of a young Pearl Bailey. She opened her big eyes as wide as she could, looked sternly at him and shook her head. She looked behind herself, looked at him once more, still shaking her head, then ran as quickly as a jackrabbit and was out of sight.

It wasn't quite sunset, but the wooded area appeared dark in the light. Papa Joe jumped off the train and tried to follow the young sister who made him think of Passion. He almost slipped, but he grabbed a tree branch and pulled himself up. As he hugged the tree, he wondered what he was running from, "What the Hell is happening back there?" he asked aloud, panting the whole time, not thinking anyone could hear him..

"We got them Gourmands good this time, that's what's going on," a deep voice behind him answered, "the whole factory's fittin' to blow. You better keep on running brother, these woods'll be burning soon."

Papa Joe turned to ask the brother if this was related to drug trafficking as well as the obvious modern day slavery, but the brother was gone in a flash. Practically in his footsteps, Papa Joe stayed on the brother's heels. He wasn't about to be found burnt up in the Mississippi woods. So he ran like he was 30 years younger, jumping over tree stumps and bushes, and swinging on heavy vines across small marshy ponds. Like the others before him he decided staying near the tracks was a wise move. As soon as a train would come he planned to hop right back on, head back to the airport, and take himself right back to Browns' Village.

He soon realized that there weren't very many people running alongside of him.—only 20 or so. The others he had seen earlier must have continued through the woods where hiding places had been previously arranged. For those who wished to escape far and quickly, the oncoming train was a gift from God. They were all grinning widely, knowing their lives had been miraculously spared.

The East Coast Express was moving at a slow 30 miles an hour since it had just left the station in Gulfport a mere 2 miles away. But it was rapidly gaining speed. Black bodies jumped from bushes and ran alongside the massive iron horse and latched themselves on to the freight cars near the caboose. The engineer blew the deep bellowing whistle at exactly the same time as the factory in Gulfport blew up. The huge BAAA ROOOM was as loud as every bomb Malik had set off all together. The impact literally shook the train that, through the prayers of it's stow-a-ways, managed to keep going. It was then followed by an outcry Papa Joe would never forget.

"THANK YA!!!!" one woman yelled up to heaven followed by another, then another.

Men were crying, kneeling and praying, hugging themselves and rocking back and forth.

"THANK YAAAA!!!" they continued for another ten minutes or so before they began to calm down and come together. Papa Joe sat amongst them, yet slightly aloof. He didn't wish to appear to be imposing. But then the woman who looked like Pearl came over to him and sat.

"Who are you, and what in the world made you come down here?"

He smiled at her heavy southern drawl, and the surprised look on her face. So he began to tell her why he was there. After explaining how Justice and Deuce were killed, he noticed that he had become the center of attention. He continued to explain to them all that they were probably related to his family in New York and how the Gourmands were attacking them all continuously. They agreed and embraced him. Each person introduced him and herself and bragged about their personal part in the uprising.

Pearl explained, "We been planning all my natural life, and I can't believe we finally did it. You see Joe, life ain't changed down here, and it sounds like it ain't no different up North. We're real sorry to hear that, 'cause that's where I always wanted to go; ain't no where else to go, white folks gonna hate us no matter where we go if we want to be free."

"That's why we gotta stick to our plan. We go north like we always said, and we deal with Mister Charlie when we get there. If he tries to make us slaves again, we blow him up again." one man said, causing them all to crack up laughing. He continued,

"We gonna change our names and get us some jobs, and vote for our own leaders. And yes Lord, we gonna have our own church!"

Papa Joe sat in tears, thinking of Browns' Village when he first got there and how the people had this same spirit of independence, strength and power. He didn't have the heart to tell him that what awaited them was a new slavery disguised in dependence on housing projects, welfare, poor education and drugs. Instead, he tried to recapture the spirit his long-distance relatives were showing him.

"As soon as y'all get to New York, all you got to do is look me up. I'll do whatever I can for you, for all of us. I think we can make our own dreams come true even though Gourmand's and other slave masters are still after us. I think we can make it."

He was looking at a little girl whose father had run through the woods with her on his back, "if we teach our children why we're here and to fight for freedom and justice, we'll be all right." They were all nodding, their eyes downcast as they reflected on his powerful words.

"You got a church preacher?" someone called out. They all laughed–especially Papa Joe. He was thinking of Reverend Franklin.

He had heard their plan and plotted his own escape. The first thing he wanted to do was getting rid of his new hat so he couldn't be confused with one of the natives; next he had to get back to the airport. Before the train pulled into the station near Jackson, his comrades jumped off and fled towards the highway, but not before sharing a multitude of hugs and kisses and well wishes.

He jumped soon after them and walked through the same train yards he had entered earlier in the heat. In disbelief, he stopped for a moment to think, trying to take it all in. He exhaled for a second, and then stopped to sit on a bench. In the stillness, he could hear the approaching frenzy. News had reached Jackson, and they were already grabbing up every Black person in sight. From a small house a few feet away, Papa Joe could hear men crying from being beaten and whipped. The sound of an actual whip hitting black skin was the ultimate for him. But he sat there and listened. He made himself listen and promised to never forget the sounds of slavery. This was when he appreciated music more than ever before–the sound of beauty and joy. He marveled at his people. "How can we make such beautiful harmony in this world that has given us so much pain?" he thought.

The wailing had ceased and he heard the white men leaving. They had been brutalizing two elderly Black men. One was After. They were trying to get them to give up the names of those who were responsible. They knew After always had the scoop, but After had been in town all day, and they couldn't prove he knew anything. So after taking their frustrations out on him and Old Sam, they gave up and just left the old men to bleed.

Papa Joe ran into the house as soon as the young hicks had gone. He found the old men in better shape than he'd expected. Apparently, they were used to being beat, and performed well enough to please their tormentors. They were shocked, though happy to see him when Joe walked in the door.

"Boy, what are you doing here?" After was trying to laugh." I remember seeing you today and wondering why in the world you picked this day to come to Jackson."

"Just let me help you out of here and I'll tell you all about it. You two are beat up pretty bad."

"It ain't no worse than they been doing all our lives." Old Sam explained. "I'm Old Sam, and that man over there is After—the last living relative of the legend Maurya herself, but you wouldn't know anything about that.

"You'd be surprised". With delight, Papa Joe told After and Old Sam about the legend he had learned of through his best friend Reverend Franklin.

"You know if you had said his name was Freeman, I would think he was a relative. We had a whole family of Freeman's escape from here after Gourmand tried to hang every one of them."

"My name is Joseph Justice Freeman," Papa Joe confessed. Then in Old Sam's car, on the way to the airport, he explained to the two old men how he and the reverend switched names in order to save his life. And in return, the two old men explained to Papa Joe how they had been planning the uprising that had taken place ever since the last Freeman; the brother of Reverend Franklin was hanged. Then they gave him the one piece of proof he needed to bury the Gourmand Empire.

Since the two old men were seen as harmless and practically useless to the whites in the factory, they were forced to perform servant and cleaning duties within the homes and offices of the factory supervisors. From the inside, they had confiscated copies of factory blue prints, lists of illegal drugs and black market cargo destined for small towns and big cities. They had copies of the drug-filled cargo and the cargo's old train and new plane schedules, and, amongst the lists of board members, affiliates, associates, political representatives and executives were the items listed as "incentives" for executives–names of indentured servants and their monetary worth. Some names came with a family history, which described family members and their attributes, like slave advertisements written a hundred years before,

"COLORED WENCH 24–28 YEARS OLD–GOOD BREEDER–$5,000.00."

Papa Joe was in shock. Proof. He had gotten actual proof.

He tried to talk the two old men into going back to Brooklyn with him, but they had their own plans. They were going fishing, fishing somewhere they would never be found.

While in the airport awaiting his flight, a rejuvenated Papa Joe sat in the airport seat staring incredulously at the vast, blue sky through the giant picture-glass window which gave the view of the entire outer airport. He stared as if he could see his old buddy waving from the heavens. His head fell back against the back top of the hardened plastic connected chair. But, he was comfortable and happy to be out of the woods. The experience had blown him away. He closed his eyes, and the revelations came. He kept seeing them–the homeless, enslaved, fearless and supposedly weak people, trudging through the dark woods towards the light. He could then see bright New York City lights in his head. It made him go back–back to 1935 and the view he used to love to drink in from the hill over the boat slip on the Hudson River. He was still new in New York City, feeling free from the whip of the ante-bellum South. But in New York City–Harlem to be exact, the freed, former southern children were in a new bondage. Papa Joe revisited the pains of the "colored" residents as his mind displayed them as if in a newsreel: men and women standing in soup lines, grown men selling apples, colored women on the corner; not selling their bodies like prostitutes, but for the same servitude they thought they had escaped. White women drove by, but occasionally stopped to hire a "girl" on the spot for a day or a week's work. Brothers ran numbers just like they would in the 1960's because they couldn't get a job—not even in Harlem. And, what else would happen but a 14-year-old "colored" boy goes into a Woolworth's Department Store and gets caught stealing. People witness the commotion when police grab him and treat him roughly. They take the boy away, and the word is spread that the white cops killed a colored boy. A riot ensued. The impoverished, denied, worn and weary destroyed the neighborhood: looting, burning, and stealing. Days later, after some Whites fled, jobs were offered, and to save themselves even Chinese laundry and restaurant owners declared that they were "colored too". The injustice was even acknowledged and pardoned by the president that time.

"But, not a damn thing has changed," he murmured to himself as the revelation continued.

Papa Joe continued his internal conversation with himself. "But look at what we can do, when we are united," he says to himself. "Here we are, seated at the bottom of the totem pole, abused and confused, but smart enough to unite to escape." He secretly prayed for his newly freed friends' safety and shakes his head in disbelief.

He jumped up when he heard "the three A.M. flight is departing from terminal six, arriving in New York City at seven-fifteen. In fifteen minutes, we will begin boarding. . ."

Papa Joe rushed to the telephone he remembered seeing before he had walked the long corridor leading to Terminal Six.

"Passion, I can't wait to tell you what I have witnessed down here."
"Pop, you all right?"
"I'm fine, baby, I'm fine. I can't wait to tell you what happened down here."

"Just come home Pops", she pleaded. "I can't rest. I need to know that you're all right."

"I can't rest either. I'm still here baby, but I'm on my way. You know ain't nothing gonna happen to Papa Joe."

She hung up laughing nervously with relief. She whispered, "Thank-you God", then collapsed in her bed, hoping to dream of Justice. She was holding on to Mecca, Zaire and Tres as they huddled together in Big Hannah's king-sized bed. She closed her eyes and saw Deuce standing before her. She reached out to embrace him and touched his bloody head, then she screamed out his name.

The next morning, Passion awoke having left the most shattering and enlightening experiences of her life. She knew where she was about to go. She hadn't escaped the boycott; and bloody cops and burning buildings from the prophetic nightmare that continued to appear before her now opened eyes. She smiled, recalling the shocked looks on white faces from seeing more black people than they had ever imagined existed in their seg-regated lives. She had seen the riot, felt the maniacal pain, heard the pierc-ing screams and she still had wanted Justice. As usual, she could feel him within her as she awakened, and the pain of loss would never shoot through her heart again because she now knew he had never left.

The yellow buses rolled across what she couldn't decipher as her mem-ory's dream or her dream's memory, as Passion sat up in bed. Her thick eyebrows fought consciousness and forced her eyes shut again. She could see Papa Joe coming home. His face was bright like Moses' after seeing the burning bush. That must have been some trip, she thought to herself. She thought of how Browns' Village must look now and knew she couldn't bear to see it, not today. She knew she needed to rest herself for the mend-ing and healing she would soon need to provide.

"RENAISSANCE"—
"BABIES FOR THE REVOLUTION"

Keisha, Mecca, Abdullah and Kareem
Tyreek and Tameeka, Shawanna, Hakiim
No more fried hair, no more shame
Not giving my baby the name of a slave
It seems like only yesterday
Heritage found was lost again

Keisha calls Mecca a "hoe" and a "bitch"
Tyreek shot Kareem 'cause he wants to be rich
Cornrows, braids or locks don't mean a damn
Brother wearing a crown is probably up to a scam
It's nothing like it was yesterday
Heritage found is lost again

Can't find a new Malcolm, Martin's unknown
Gotta sell drugs if you want a throne
Silly little rappers want to be "The Mack"
while the little lost girls think it's "phat" and "all that"
to wear tight minis and platform shoes,
ride in fancy cars and not go to school
It's a dirty, rotten, low-down shame
Heritage found is lost again

"Nigger" has risen like Lazarus from the dead
"We say it with love" is commonly said
Little brother has become the once dreaded "man"

He's more likely to lynch you than "skin-heads" or the klan
Steal your car, mug you in broad daylight
Give a share to his mama, she makes it all right
The nightmare lives with us, the dream a lost friend
Heritage found is lost again

Who's gonna take the weight—let's see
Who wasn't killed, who didn't flee?
Who didn't become the enemy?
Who cares about more than just "me", "me", "me"?
If ancestors whose names that are bared
could be heard, rest assure they'd give us the word.
Maybe love, we will then comprehend
So heritage lost could be found again.

                                        Cathie Lewis

Chapter Ten

▼

"Renaissance"

BROWNS' VILLAGE
July 4, 2000

Justice Freeman III stood before the Justice Freeman Community Center with his Quarter and Pat, both holding a luggage cart filled with cans of paint. He gripped their small shoulders tightly, his eyes fixed on the ghostly mural of his one-handed djembe playing daddy, and the arms of his loving mother, outstretched on either side of the drummer to welcome all. Faded beyond recognition to most, it was vibrantly visible to anyone who had been there to witness the magic of love, to witness Justice and Passion.

The little boys looked up at their father strangely, "Daddy, you all right?"

Young Justice, like his grandmother Passion wasn't afraid to say what he felt, or what he saw. He also had Passion's beautiful eyes, which made Tres slip into the past almost every time he looked at his eldest boy.

Just as Tres attempted to open his mouth to explain what he was feeling to the concerned two, Brother Paul, now the caretaker of the community center opened the door and ran out to greet the family.

"I'm so happy that you agreed to come back and speak on your parent's behalf. I've been trying to get folks back in this center for years, but I guess it's gonna take Justice and Passion to work the magic.

"I'm glad to be back Brother Paul. I was very surprised to hear from you. I came because I know that my parents would have wanted me to do this–Papa Joe too. And I can't even reflect on a day in my childhood with-out thinking of Mama Lettie and how much love she gave us. You know Brother, I didn't realize that she wasn't my real grandmother until she died ten years ago and her family showed up and told their history. She sin-cerely loved us as if her blood ran through our veins. Her love was always so...real, so...." Tres was desperately trying to come up with a phrase to describe the secure and nurtured sense Mama Lettie had made him feel. Then he realized that it wasn't just her.

"It was just her though," the revelation manifested, "Miss Connie, Miss Anne, Miss Hannah, old Miss Lucy, Reverend Mitchell, my Papa Joe and all of the afro-wearing brothers, Mr. Pete–man, everybody–everybody made this a village. And together with my immediate family, they all gave me strength and security as well as love."

Tres was speaking to Brother Paul, but he was so filled with emotion, he was speaking rather loudly and had drawn the attention of people walking towards Sutter Avenue. Many were curious because he seemed to be preaching without a soapbox; others were wondering what was up with all of the paint. A few elders thought they recognized him and decided to confront him.

"What's your name son?" They spoke in unison with raised eyebrows.

Despite the attention, he couldn't help but to let the spirit flow. He had heard their question, but couldn't stop. Tres was on a roll and his past was flashing before his eyes. He was now completely overwhelmed with the emptiness that had enveloped his beloved home. Bus stop signs for the express to Riker's Island Penitentiary and crack houses were the new exclusive features; there were no remnants of The Dew Drop Inn, Pete's Barber Shop, the bakery and luncheonette. It reduced him to uncontrollable tears.

"Look at us now!," like Malcolm standing on a makeshift stage, he began again. "We're so afraid of each other that people who grew up here won't even come back to visit."

"I don't blame them,' the elder who recognized him said. "I'm scared to come out of my apartment at night. Sometimes I think they're gonna shoot me right through the front door like they did my grandson five years ago. This neighborhood ain't no community no more. It's just one big jail. And the drug dealers and the cops are the guards."

People nodded and murmured," she's right, she's right."

"I know it's bad here. But it's not like we don't know why. We know who is responsible and we know why they've been successful. Drug trafficking has disabled us. But the question is, what are we going to do about it?!"

Tres had begun to yell before he realized that he was raising his voice in competition of an approaching 2000 Navigator armed with woofers the size of a person which drowned out Tres' voice with ease. Everyone stopped and watched the drug mobile as it literally vibrated to its excessively amplified bass. The driver laughed as it sped through the red light knowing he had disturbed everyone's peace.

"It's them—we need to kill 'em all!" The elder's voice was trembling.

"Maybe they're already dead Ma." His point made everyone think. "You know what I really believe the answer has to be?" He allowed a little time to elapse to get the crowd's attention, "new life and a new birth. Folks, we need a renaissance."

They questioned one another, "renaissance?"

Then, "Yeah! I'm feeling that!" The crowd burst into laughter. The "hip-hop" vernacular had danced out of an old woman's mouth.

"Since when do you talk about *feeling* something Miss Shirley?" Brother Paul was laughing as he kidded the eighty-two year old lady he did handy work for anytime he had the chance.

"Shoot. My great-grand taught me all that stuff. We be 'illin all the time." The crowd was rolling. "But this young man is right. We definitely need a renaissance." People were nodding in agreement and affirming the change approaching in the cycle of their life. "Are you the son of Justice?" she asked and searched his eyes intensely.

"Yes." His voice was deep and calm. He tilted his head, smiled and stared back, entranced by her plunge into the windows of his soul.

Tres was beginning to feel like the son of Justice again. He hadn't felt that way in a long time. A hero's son. And now the hero himself, sounding like his grandfather, the reverend.

"I don't know about you, but I don't want my sons to grow up thinking that drug dealing is the only way to make money, or that it is moral or righteous to live a world where destroying your own brother is accept-able. I want my sons to know the real inheritance that has been passed down to us."

He turned to his sons, knelt before them and explained,

"We are not people who give up. We don't jump ship and we don't turn our backs on our community. My mother, father, brother, uncles and grandparents all died right here trying to make it a better place. And, although the enemy has divided us and conquered us over and over again, we keep fighting back. And, we're still here! The people who live behind these project walls are people of God—people who have the right to live well, live free and peacefully, and to live happily. And, we have been given the capacity to help them do that. We possess the power and strength of our ancestors and our history. We possess the creativity to make things look beautiful, and to play the music that uplifts people's hearts. But most of all, you know what we have?"

The boys were shaking their heads slowly; their eyes were riveted.

"We have the power of love. This is the only thing that supercedes all of the things that can enslave us. So I want you both to promise me that you will always love God, yourselves, your ancestors and your people. And if you do, love will be given back to you."

The crowd was in tears. Tres sharing this personal moment with his home community was the spark they all needed to change their hearts towards hope.

"Can we begin to change things right here and make the Justice Freeman Community Center, the Browns' Village Renaissance Center?" He was challenging the unsuspecting participants.

"Yeah!"

"I'm down with that!"

Voices came out of the air; a consensus of village representatives began calling children and neighbors from below.

"Come downstairs! Come down now!"
"What's going on?" they all wanted to know.

Tres let out a long exhale after a 30 second inhalation through his nostrils, "We can do this y'all," he smiled looking like Justice. He glanced over at Brother Paul and started nodding his head as if he had just been given a great idea.

"And the one man who could inspire us all the most right now is standing right next to me. I'm sure everyone knows, or thinks they know Brother Paul here. To you, he is a reliable porter–the project handy man. But Brother and my family have a history that goes back way before he started working for Housing. I'm going to let him tell his story."

Brother the junkie a.k.a. Brother Paul stepped towards Tres with tears in his eyes, secretly, he had always prayed for an opportunity to take it all back, to beg forgiveness for the evil he had done. He stood before the crowd, the wall-less church, behind an imaginary podium and began to testify, confessing his forty-year-old sins.
"I guess it's time to testify,"

He struggled to look into the faces of the people who would soon see him in a very different light.

"But before I do, I ask that you all remember the story of the escaped slave Maurya many of us learned about as children. And remember that everything negative that we have suffered in this country began when the first slave set foot in America. And before you judge me by my mistakes, please try to understand my experience has taught me that like Maurya, instead of destroying ourselves, we must learn to endure the suffering until we are given another opportunity to escape. The things I have done, and the way that I used to live will shock you, but then you'll understand why I believe we can change all of these confused young brothers with some passion, justice, and some new paint."

Dr. Justice Freeman III stood next to the changed Brother, then at his sons, then at the faces wearing amazement and awe. Then he envisioned a beautiful mural filled with ancestors and children.

THE END

AFTERWORD

heritage would be more than just a word,
more than stories of strangers that seem so absurd
but a way of living, giving directions to those on the front lines the
ancestors chose.

C. Wright-Lewis 4/16/94

0-595-19576-8